Great-Grandma reached over and took Sabrina's hand.

"When you find that wishdust, Sabrina . . . and I have great confidence that you will . . . I'll take it off your hands. I'll take it to the Witch Council. Along with the woman who gave it to you. In a fishbowl. She won't get away with this, dear . . . I'll see to it."

"Well . . . thanks, Great-Grandma. For the encouragement, at least."

"You're welcome, dear. You just focus your attention on that wishdust, use all the resources available to you, and don't stop until you've found it. Or until it destroys civilization as you know it. Whichever comes first."

Sabrina, the Teenage Witch™ books

Available from ARCHWAY Paperbacks

Sabrina The Teenage Witch™

All That Glitters

Ray Garton

AN ARCHWAY PAPERBACK
Published by POCKET BOOKS
New York London Toronto Sydney Tokyo Singapore

This book is a work of fiction. Names, characters, places and incidents are products of the author's imagination or are used fictitiously. Any resemblance to actual events or locales or persons living or dead is entirely coincidental.

AN ARCHWAY PAPERBACK *Original*

An Archway Paperback published by
POCKET BOOKS, a division of Simon & Schuster Inc.
1230 Avenue of the Americas, New York, NY 10020

ISBN: 0-671-02116-8

First Archway Paperback printing July 1998

10 9 8 7 6 5 4 3 2 1

AN ARCHWAY PAPERBACK and colophon are registered trademarks of Simon & Schuster Inc.

SABRINA THE TEENAGE WITCH and all related titles, logos and characters are trademarks of Archie Comics Publications, Inc.

Printed in the U.S.A.

IL: 5+

This book is dedicated to

Don Geronimo
and
Mike O'Meara

Radio gods who always make
my tears turns to laughter!

and to

my wonderful wife,
Dawn

All That Glitters

☆

Chapter 1

☆

Sabrina looked forward to Sunday mornings. Five days a week, she had to get up early so she wouldn't be late for her first class at school. There was no school on Saturday, of course, but it always seemed to be an active day, and something or other usually got her out of bed early. Sundays, on the other hand, were for sleeping in. They were long, slow, lazy days, so there was never any hurry to get started. When she awoke on Sunday mornings, Sabrina always reached over and turned her radio on, then rolled over leisurely and went back to sleep.

This particular Sunday morning was different.

"Time to wake up!" Aunt Zelda said cheerfully.

"A-bargain-hunting we will go!" Aunt Hilda declared.

Sabrina was lying facedown in bed, snuggled under her covers. She lifted her face from her pillow and stared blearily at her headboard. Mumbling to herself, she decided she'd been dreaming. Without even looking, she reached over and turned on the radio on her bedstand, then snuggled under the covers again.

"Sabrina!" Aunt Zelda said, raising her voice. "Come on, dear, get up! We're going on a little adventure."

"Yes!" Aunt Hilda agreed. "Someplace you've never been. And you're going to love it."

Sabrina felt a sudden weight on her feet, and Salem's voice joined in. "Don't make me come over there and lick your face."

Sabrina stirred beneath the covers and mumbled into her pillow, "That . . . wasn't . . . a dream."

"You're not dreaming," Salem said. "You're just not getting up."

Sabrina slowly sat up in bed, yawned, rubbed her sleepy eyes with her knuckles, and looked at her aunts. She blinked a few times, then rubbed her eyes again. She couldn't believe what she was seeing.

Aunt Zelda and Aunt Hilda were sharp dressers. They were very picky about the clothes they wore and the way they did their hair and makeup. The two women standing in Sabrina's bedroom did not look like her aunts.

They both wore faded, threadbare jeans with nearly worn-through knees and baggy old sweat-shirts that had seen better days. Kerchiefs covered their hair—a blue one for Zelda, a red one for Hilda—and each of them had a pair of large, round sunglasses pushed up over her kerchief.

"Are you two going to a costume party, or something?" Sabrina asked, frowning.

"No, dear," Aunt Zelda said. "We're going to the Rummage Realm!"

Aunt Hilda clapped her hands together and said, "That's right! And we're taking you with us!"

"And me!" Salem said, jumping into Aunt Hilda's arms.

"You're taking me . . . *where?*" Sabrina asked.

"We don't have time to explain now," Aunt Zelda said. "Just get up and shower and put on your grungies. We'll tell you all about it on the way."

They both grinned down at her excitedly, their eyes bright.

Salem said, "Come on, Sabrina. They've never taken me, either, and I want to go!"

Sabrina swung her legs over the edge of the bed, stood slowly, and stretched. Then she peered out the window. There was no sunlight.

"Hey," she said, her voice hoarse. "It's still dark outside!"

"Well, if we don't get there early," Aunt Hilda said, "everything will be picked over!"

"That's right," Aunt Zelda said. "The best buys are always snatched up right away!" She clapped her hands hard three times. "Chop-chop! Into the shower!"

"Okay, okay," Sabrina said, grabbing her robe. "But this better be good."

Twenty minutes later Sabrina was showered and dressed. She wore old jeans and a black sweatshirt she hadn't taken from her closet in over a year. It had a huge yellow smiley face on the front, tattered cuffs at the end of sleeves, and she hated it . . . but it was the grungiest thing she could come up with. She stood before her aunts and Salem in her old clothes and messy hair.

"I can't go out in public like this!" she cried. "I look . . . well . . . *skanky!*"

"We *all* look skanky, dear!" Aunt Zelda said with great enthusiasm.

"Wait a second." Aunt Hilda turned to her sister. "What's *skanky?* It sounds disgusting."

"It means we *look* disgusting," Aunt Zelda replied.

"Oh, well, yes," Aunt Hilda said, turning to Sabrina with a smile. "Of course we look disgusting! Normally, we wouldn't be caught dead looking this way!"

4

"That's right," Aunt Zelda said. "But everybody dresses like this to go to the Rummage Realm."

"The *what?*" Sabrina asked.

"The Rummage Realm!" Salem replied. He was perched on the edge of Sabrina's bed and his tail flicked about excitedly. "I've never been, but . . . I've heard there's a booth there that sells Lizard Flakes."

"And they're *full* of cholesterol, Salem," Aunt Zelda chided.

Sabrina's face screwed into a look of dread. "You mean . . . you're taking me someplace where it's okay for my hair to look like . . . *this?*"

"Don't worry," Aunt Hilda said. She reached into her pocket and removed a green kerchief. "We'll cover it with this."

Uh-oh, Sabrina thought. *Maybe, when they aren't looking, I can zap this into a baseball cap.*

"Won't I need an umbrella?" Sabrina asked as Aunt Hilda finished tying the kerchief in the back of her head. It had been very rainy lately, and Sabrina didn't want to get soaked.

"Oh, no, dear," Aunt Zelda said. "It won't be raining where we're going."

Aunt Hilda took Sabrina's arm and said, "Come on, come on, we don't want to be late."

"Late for what?" Sabrina asked as they left her bedroom and went into the hall.

"Hey!" Salem called, chasing after them. "You're not leaving me behind again!"

They went across the hall and stopped in front of the linen closet.

"Oh," Sabrina said, turning to her aunts. "So . . . this really is another realm? I thought you wanted to go to a rummage sale, or something."

"It is a rummage sale!" Aunt Zelda said excitedly. "But for *witches!*"

"Yes," Aunt Hilda said, clutching her hands together. "It's like an enormous, glorious flea market just for witches, with everything a witch could ever hope to find . . . and always at a bargain!"

"But it's very dusty there," Aunt Zelda said. "We'll get dirty, but . . . we'll get some good buys!"

Salem looked up at them and asked, "Is someone going to carry me, or do I have to slog through the dust and get my fur all dirty? Remember . . . *I* don't get to put on my grungies."

Sabrina smiled. "I'll carry you, Salem," she said, bending down to pick him up in her arms.

"Well, are we all ready?" Aunt Hilda asked.

"I'm ready!" Aunt Zelda replied.

"I can't *wait!*" Salem said.

Sabrina took in a deep breath and let it out

slowly. "Welllll," she said, "I don't know if I'm ready, but . . . let's go."

Aunt Hilda opened the closet door and they all stepped inside.

Lights flashed.

Towels fluttered.

Then the closet was empty again.

☆

Chapter 2

☆

The thing that amazed Sabrina most about the Rummage Realm was its size, its vastness. Once they passed through the enormous wrought-iron gate, Sabrina stood and stared at the sight before her.

Everything was spread out on an endlessly flat, dusty plain. There were clumps of trees here and there . . . tall, fat-trunked trees with green bark and large, clover-shaped purple leaves dangling from their tentaclelike branches. The fine dirt beneath their feet was the color of old pennies, and with each step, a little dusty cloud puffed up around the foot.

There were two small suns in the sky, one to the east and one to the west. Neither was terribly bright, but that might have been because of the cloud cover. The clouds filled most of the sky and looked like giant scoops of vanilla ice cream with strawberry swirls. In the gaps between the clouds, Sabrina could see a sky of cotton-candy pink.

"Wow," Sabrina said as she looked out over the plain. It was teeming with people walking among open tables, enclosed booths, and colorful tents and kiosks. "This place is . . . *big!*"

"Enormous," Aunt Hilda said. "You couldn't cover everything here if you spent all day!"

"Of course you could, Hilda," Aunt Zelda said.

Aunt Hilda frowned a moment. "Oh, that's right. I forgot . . . night never falls here. The two suns just trade places."

"You mean, it's always daytime here?" Sabrina asked. "This is *always* going on?"

Aunt Zelda nodded. "That's right. But we only come here once a year, or so. That's about how often new vendors come along with new wares to sell."

"And if we came here more often than that," Aunt Hilda added, "we'd be broke."

"Are we going to stand here and chat?" Salem asked. "Or are we going shopping?"

They went shopping.

Once they were among the milling crowds of people going from table to table and booth to booth, Sabrina caught the smells of some of the foods available for sale. The mix of aromas was

9

rich and exotic and made Sabrina realize she hadn't eaten breakfast. Everything around her was so fascinating, though, that she was able to forget her hunger for the time being.

Wandering among the bargain hunters were clowns with brightly painted faces. One of them even rode an enormous lizardlike animal that had a beak and two feathered wings folded against its sides. The clown wore a sandwich-board sign that read "Have Your Picture Taken on the Flying Lizard!"

"Hey," Sabrina said to her aunts, "what's that tent over there? It looks like a fortune-teller's tent, or something."

"A fortune-teller?" Aunt Zelda asked, shaking her head. "At a flea market for witches? That would be silly. Fortune-tellers are entertaining to *mortals* . . . but witches really have no use for them."

Sabrina nodded. "That makes sense. So . . . what *is* in that tent over there?"

Aunt Hilda leaned close to Sabrina and said, "That tent is here every year, and it's much more entertaining than a fortune-teller. You see . . . once you've paid the admission, you get to go into the tent and watch a mortal balance his checkbook with nothing more than a calculator and whatever he can remember from his math classes back in school."

Sabrina frowned, but Salem began to laugh in her arms.

"We should check that out before we leave, Sabrina," the cat said. "That sounds hilarious!"

"Uh . . . sure," Sabrina said.

Sabrina followed her aunts over to a table covered with beautiful, multicolored, delicate-looking shawls. On closer inspection, Sabrina found the shawls to be much heavier than they looked. The woman behind the table was very short and very round, with white hair and large bright eyes. She wore a shawl exactly like those she was selling.

"Hello, ladies!" the short, squat woman chirped in a high, birdlike voice. "Do you like what you see?"

"Oh, yes," Aunt Zelda said, "these shawls are lovely."

Sabrina wrinkled her nose. The shawls *were* beautiful, but she couldn't exactly wear one to school.

Aunt Hilda leaned forward and asked, "But, uh . . . what do they do?"

"They help you fly!" the woman said. She waved both pudgy hands and said, "If you wear one of these while you're in flight, you won't have to put out nearly as much energy, because with these shawls, you can coast! In other words . . . they'll cut down on your mileage like you wouldn't believe!"

11

Sabrina's aunts began to discuss which of the shawls they wanted to buy. Meanwhile, Sabrina's stomach continued to growl and grumble.

"Um, I'm hungry," Sabrina said. "I haven't had breakfast."

"Oh, of course!" Aunt Zelda said. "Hilda and I had a bite back at the house, but we were so eager to get here, we completely forgot about breakfast for *you,* dear!" She removed some money from the pocket of her jeans and handed a few bills to Sabrina. "Here you go, sweetie. There are a couple of food stands right over there," she said with a nod. "You go have some breakfast. Hilda and I will be heading that way"—she waved her hand in the direction they would be going—"so you shouldn't have any problem finding us. Get something to eat and do some shopping, if you like." She smiled, patted Sabrina on the cheek, then went back to discussing flying shawls with her sister.

"Well, I guess it's just you and me, Salem," Sabrina said as she turned and walked away from her aunts with the cat in her arms.

"It could be worse," Salem said. "It could be just *me.* This place is too crowded. I'd be roadkill in no time."

Salem was thrilled when they found a food kiosk selling bowls of Lizard Flakes. Sabrina ordered a couple of fruit-kabobs . . . pieces of various fruits from Alpha Centauri speared on two long, thin sticks. They ate at a round wooden table in front of the kiosk, Sabrina sitting on a bench and Salem on the tabletop eating his Lizard Flakes out of a Styrofoam bowl.

Salem finished first, and as he licked his whiskers and washed his face with his paws, he said quietly, "Oh, that was so good . . . delicious, absolutely delicious. . . ."

When they were both done, Sabrina took Salem in to her arms, and they went back into the crowded marketplace. They were heading in the direction of Aunt Zelda and Aunt Hilda when Sabrina saw a display of beautiful jewelry that she simply could not pass up. She had a lot of rings, but was always on the lookout for other pieces. As she looked over the jewelry, the man behind the table told her that each piece, when worn, enhanced spells. They were way out of her price range, but beautiful to look at . . . just like the beautiful assortment of "air-walking" shoes at the next table . . . and the line of magical beauty products at the next table.

Time passed quickly as Sabrina and Salem went from table to table, chatting, looking over the wares. The day wore on, and the two suns in the cotton-candy-pink sky with the vanilla-and-strawberry-swirl clouds slowly made their way toward changing places.

Each item for sale had some element of magic to it that would make life easier for the common witch—flying shawls, potion supplements, finger exercisers—and Sabrina was fascinated by it all. She kept saying things to Salem like, "Isn't this *amazing?"* and, "Can you *believe* this?"

"Look," Salem said finally, "I've been a witch a lot longer than you have." He paused a moment, and they looked at each other silently. Salem sighed and bobbed his head back and forth. "Okay, okay, I've been a *cat* for a long time, too. But I've been a witch a lot longer than that . . . and I've seen all this stuff. So you'll pardon me if I don't find it so amazing."

"Well, I do find it amazing," Sabrina said. "It's like being in a toy store . . . but all the toys look and work exactly as they do on the commercials . . . even better!"

"Mind if I ask a favor?" Salem asked. "We've been looking at shoes and clothes and jewelry and magical hair barrettes that always keep your hair perfectly in place for so long, now . . . do you think we could do something I want to do?"

"Sure, Salem. What would you like to do? Are you hungry again? You want some more Lizard Flakes?"

"Not yet." Salem cocked his head mischievously. "I want to go see the mortal trying to balance his checkbook!"

Sabrina looked at the cat with narrowed eyes and a smirk. "And after that, can we go on looking at all the tables and booths?"

"Sure!" Salem replied, perking up.

They went over to the tent, paid the admission, and went inside.

About ten minutes later, they came out again. On the way out, Sabrina rolled her eyes, and Salem buried his face in her shoulder as he quaked with laughter.

"I didn't find that very entertaining at all," Sabrina said. "It was just some poor guy sitting in his house trying to balance his checkbook, which isn't always as easy as it sounds."

Salem leaned his head back and bellowed out more laughter. "Oh, come on," he said, after gathering his composure. "It's not that hard. You want hard? Waiting for a mouse to come out from under a dresser . . . now *that's* hard, *that* takes skill and patience. That guy balancing his checkbook . . . he was so confused, I thought his head was going to explode!" He started rocking with laughter again in Sabrina's arms.

"Hey! Don't forget, Salem . . . I'm half mortal."

"So, when you have to balance a checkbook, you can do half with magic . . . and half the hard way!" Once again, Salem burst into laughter.

Sabrina sighed and shook her head as she carried Salem back into the crowd to do some more browsing in the Rummage Realm.

Chapter 3

Sabrina found a lot of things that interested her enough to spend time looking at them. Sometimes she even asked questions about them of the salespeople. Most of the items, however interesting, were out of her price range, and even those things she could afford, she simply didn't need. That was okay, though; she realized she was having a lot more fun than she thought she'd be having when she was dragged out of bed by her aunts before sunrise on a Sunday morning.

When Sabrina and Salem saw the brightly colored tent, they almost walked past it. It was covered with swirls of maroon and purple and yellow and green . . . colors that should have clashed, but which looked beautiful on the tent's canvas.

Before they could pass the tent, Salem said, "Hey, look."

Sabrina stopped and looked at the tent again. A rectangular sign was dancing in the air in front of the tent. It read:

WISHES GRANTED
INQUIRE WITHIN

"Goofy sign," Sabrina said.

Salem nodded. "Yeah . . . what do you suppose it means . . . 'Wishes granted'?"

"It probably means if you go inside the tent and lay down your money, somebody grants you a wish," Salem said. "Maybe it's a genie."

"But why would witches need to have their wishes granted? It doesn't make sense."

"We could always go inside and find out."

"You think we should?" Sabrina asked, frowning slightly at Salem.

"Well, of course we should!" the cat said, rolling his eyes. "That's why we're here!"

Sabrina walked over to the tent and cautiously pulled aside the flap.

In the back of the small tent sat an old woman who looked impossibly old. She was flanked by a number of floating globes that glowed with a soft, eerie gold light. She was sitting Indian-style on a stack of pillows and her head was bowed, peering at something in her lap. There was a small, low table in front of her, and on the other side of it were more pillows. She was alone . . . except for the animal at her side. It was the ugliest, weirdest-looking creature Sabrina had ever seen in her life.

"What . . . is that?" Salem whispered in her ear.

"I don't know," Sabrina whispered back.

"Well," Salem said with an audible gulp and a shudder, "I'm gonna have nightmares about it for weeks!"

The old woman lifted her head suddenly. She smiled when she saw Sabrina, revealing gums that held only a few scattered yellowed teeth in her head.

"Aaahhh," the old woman said in a low, scratchy voice. "Someone who wants to make her wishes come true."

Salem pressed his nose to Sabrina's ear and whispered, "Let's get outta here, okay?"

Sabrina nodded. She smiled at the old woman and said, "Sorry, I, uh . . . I think I got the wrong tent, that's all, I just—"

In spite of her frail, bony appearance, the old woman rose to her feet with incredible agility and hurried over to Sabrina. She took Sabrina's hand in hers and said, "Don't be afraid, sweetie. You've come to the right place, all right. C'mon in, have a seat. Bring your kitty in and make yourself comfortable." She tugged on Sabrina's hand.

Sabrina couldn't bring herself to be rude. She glanced at Salem with a "so-what-do-you-want-*me*-to-do" expression, and allowed the old woman to pull her into the tent.

"Uh, well," Sabrina said, "we were just curious about the floating sign outside, that's all. What does it mean?"

"It means exactly what it says, dear. Here, have a seat on the pillows."

Salem's eyes never wavered from the odd creature behind the small table. "Don't get too close to that thing!" Salem whispered to her.

The creature had a catlike head with gray and charcoal stripes and long white whiskers. It had the body of a large white duck, a long snakelike tail, and the talons of a large bird of prey.

"Oh, don't mind him," the old woman said, returning to her seat beside the strange animal. "He won't hurt you. He's a pussycat."

"I beg your pardon!" Salem blurted. "Parts of him might bear a resemblance, but, I mean, *really*—!"

Sabrina gently hushed Salem as she sat on the pillows. In spite of what the old woman said about her pet, Sabrina kept a cautious eye on it.

"You want your wishes granted, young lady?" the old woman asked.

"Uh . . . well, I just kinda wanted to know what you were selling."

The old woman reached beneath the small table and produced a mottled, leathery pouch closed at the top with a thick drawstring. She placed the pouch on the table and looked at Sabrina, as if waiting for a reaction.

"That's an unusual, uh . . . change purse," Sabrina said.

"This is no change purse," the old woman said. "It's just a pouch made of genuine pleather—plastic leather. What's important is what the pouch *holds.*"

"Marbles?" Salem guessed.

She ignored him. "It holds . . . *wishdust!*" she said dramatically.

Sabrina frowned slightly. "Wish . . . dust?"

The old woman pushed the pouch toward Sabrina with a knobby-knuckled hand and said, "Go ahead, open it up and take a look."

Sabrina started to put Salem down on the pillow next to her, but he whispered fiercely, "If you put me down, I swear, I'll scream."

She continued to hold him as she lifted the bag and pried it open with thumb and forefinger. In the soft golden light of the floating globes, Sabrina had to bring the open pouch close to her face to see inside. It was a little over half-full of what appeared to be glitter . . . multicolored, iridescent glitter.

"Well?" the old woman said, dragging the word out.

"It's very pretty," Sabrina said. "But it's just glitter. I could get some at the local craft store."

The old woman cackled. "No, no, not just glitter." She reached over the table and took the pouch back. She took a pinch of the glittery powder between her thumb and forefinger, closed her eyes and said quietly, "I wish I had a big bouquet of fragrant roses." She scattered the glitter into the air and it fell in a sparkling, dusty cloud to the table. The second it hit the surface, it was gone, and a lovely vase of roses appeared. The old woman bared the remains of her teeth in a grin. "See? That's why it's called wishdust . . . because it makes wishes come true."

"But I could've done that with a wave of my hand," Sabrina said. She was being polite, but she didn't see why the old woman was making such a big deal about her wishdust.

"Yes, you could have, dear," the old woman said. "But then it would be *your* magic. *Your* energy."

"And that would mean . . . what?" Sabrina asked.

"That would mean you'd be expending energy

unnecessarily, putting forth an effort when you didn't need to. As the mortals say, dear . . . don't sweat the small stuff. You could be using wishdust, instead!"

"Well, it's interesting, but I—"

"Are you familiar with the ways of mortals, sweetie?" the old woman asked.

Sabrina chuckled. "Vaguely."

Salem whispered in her ear, "I want to become familiar with the outside of this tent again, really soon, okay?"

Sabrina saw the cat-headed creature waddling slowly around the table toward them. It was looking at Salem very curiously.

Salem stiffened in Sabrina's arms and his fur bristled as he glared down at the approaching creature. "Hey, hey," Salem said, trying to sound firm, but only sounding afraid, "don't make me come down there, okay?"

The cat-headed duck creature stopped about a foot away from Sabrina, still looking up at Salem.

"I'm telling you," Salem said tremulously, "my claws are a *lot* bigger than you might think!"

"I'm sorry if you find my appearance disturbing," the creature said with a strange accent. "I'm not going to hurt you. And I can assure you that you look just as weird to me as I do to you."

"Oh, fat chance of *that!*" Salem huffed.

"Come on down here and let's talk while they do business. I won't bite."

"Being bitten by you is only one of my concerns."

"My name is Larimus, by the way. And you are . . . ?"

Salem cautiously left the crook of Sabrina's arm and stood before the bizarre creature named Larimus.

"I'm Salem. If, uh, you don't mind my asking, Larimus . . . what *are* you?"

"Well, I was once a cat . . . but that was centuries ago. So long ago that I'd forgotten what a cat looks like. That's why you looked kind of odd to me."

"What happened to you?"

"I was a familiar for a couple of witches. They were married . . . for a while. Then they got a divorce and I got caught in the middle of an ugly custody battle and . . . here I am."

While Salem and Larimus chatted, the old woman continued. "Mortals have a way of getting around effort, my dear. They invented electric can openers so they wouldn't have to twist the handle on the manual models. Easier, faster, more efficient . . . and all with less effort. Well, the wishdust is nothing more than an electric can opener for witches."

Sabrina smiled. She wasn't quite convinced about the wishdust, but she had to admit the old woman was making some sense.

"How do I know it will work for me?" Sabrina asked.

"Try it!" The old woman handed the pouch back to Sabrina.

Sabrina took a pinch of wishdust from the pouch. She stopped to think about a wish.

"You don't have to say it out loud," the old woman said. "Just *think* your wish."

"Hey," Salem said, turning to Sabrina. "You're making a wish? How about a bag of Lizard Flakes?"

"That's a brand-name product, Salem," Sabrina said. "You know witches can't conjure brand names."

"Witches can't," the old woman said, "but wishdust *can*. Remember . . . it won't be your magic. It'll be the wishdust doing the work."

Sabrina shrugged with one shoulder, then sprinkled the dust in the air . . . and a bag of Lizard Flakes appeared on the table before her with a smiling cartoon cat on the front.

"Wow!" Salem exclaimed. He jumped onto the table and began to circle the bag. "This is the real thing! Thank you, Sabrina!"

Sabrina stared at the box in wide-eyed, open-mouthed amazement. "How did I do that?" she muttered. "I don't know what a bag of Lizard Flakes looks like, or . . . or . . ."

"You didn't do it," the old woman said. She wore a satisfied smile. "The wishdust did it . . . just as I said it would. It doesn't matter that you've never seen something before. The wishdust will come up with whatever you wish for . . . whenever you wish for it."

"And brand names, too!" Sabrina exclaimed. "My magic can't even do that." She remembered the time she conjured up Roller-blahs.

Salem jumped from the table and into Sabrina's lap. "Oh, please get some, please get some, please-please-please-*please!* Zelda and Hilda never get these for me! They say they're too fattening! You can wish up Lizard Flakes anytime. And, uh . . . well, you know . . . stuff for *you,* too."

Sabrina was surprised to find that she was suddenly very interested in the wishdust. Maybe it *was* everything the old woman said it was . . . maybe it *was* like an electric can opener for witches.

The old woman leaned over and plucked the pouch from Sabrina's hand. "Would you be interested in a pouch of wishdust, sweetie?" she asked.

Salem fidgeted on Sabrina's lap as he said, "Don't make me beg."

"You *are* begging," Sabrina said.

"Well, don't make me beg more, then!"

"I don't know, Salem. I think I should talk to Aunt Zelda and Aunt Hilda first."

"Are you kidding? They're no fun! They'll blow it!"

"I'm sure I don't have enough money on me," Sabrina pointed out. "I should talk to them first."

"But . . . you *are* interested?" Salem asked.

"Yes, very interested." Sabrina smiled at the old woman.

Salem hopped off her lap and muttered to himself, "Oh, goodie-goodie-goodie!"

On the other side of the table, the old woman held up the pouch and said, "This is my last one. I've just been waiting for someone to buy it so I can fold up my tent and go home. If you go talk to your aunts, I can't guarantee you I'll be here when you get back."

"Oh . . . really?" Sabrina nibbled on her lower lip thoughtfully. "Well . . . how much do you want for that pouch of wishdust?"

The old woman smiled, leaned forward and rested her elbows on the table, holding the pouch between her gnarled hands. "Let's negotiate, dear. How much do you have?"

While Sabrina negotiated with the old woman, Salem hopped onto the table and knocked the bag of Lizard Flakes to the floor. He went to

Larimus's side and asked, "Ever had Lizard Flakes?"

"No, I'm afraid not. Are they good?"

"Good? Hah! They're *incredible!* Let's open this baby up . . . you're gonna love 'em!" Salem tore the top of the bag open with his claws and the brown and beige cat snacks tumbled out. "Chow down!"

Chapter 4

☆

By the time Sabrina, her aunts, and Salem walked out of the linen closet and back into the house, they were exhausted by a long day of shopping in the Rummage Realm.

"It's still light outside," Sabrina said, glancing at a window. "I thought it would be dark by now."

"Oh, no," Aunt Zelda said. "The sun's just coming up."

"We've only been gone half-an-hour at this end," Aunt Hilda said, heading downstairs. "Different time zones."

"Way different," Sabrina said. As she put Salem down on the floor, she asked her aunts, "Hey, didn't you two buy anything?"

"Are you kidding?" Aunt Hilda said with

chuckle. "If we'd stayed any longer, there wouldn't be anything left in that realm!"

"We sent everything ahead," Aunt Zelda said, kicking off her shoes.

Sabrina followed her aunts into the kitchen with Salem on her heels. She gasped, and said, "Good grief! You *did* buy a lot!"

The kitchen table was buried beneath boxes and bags and contraptions and stacks of books.

"We're gonna need a bigger house," Salem said, shaking his head.

"It's not as much as it looks," Aunt Zelda said. "It's all easily stored."

Salem looked over the mountain of merchandise and asked, "But . . . what is it?"

"A little bit everything!" Aunt Hilda said happily. She and Aunt Zelda took turns describing their treasures.

They'd picked up all the latest bestselling spell books written by some of the biggest names in magic. Aunt Zelda bought some new equipment for her Lab-Top and Aunt Hilda bought jars and jars of ingredients for potions and spells, and racks to hold them. There were magic games for family gatherings, invisibility hats, flying shawls, and hover shoes for when you don't want to land, but you don't really want to keep flying, either. There was more, too . . . much more.

"What about you, Sabrina?" Aunt Zelda asked when she and her sister were finished. "Didn't you buy anything? Wasn't there anything you or Salem wanted?"

"I got a bag of Lizard Flakes!" Salem said excitedly.

"Where are they?" Aunt Hilda asked.

"Well, uh . . . Larimus and I ate 'em."

Aunt Zelda said, "Salem, how many times have I told you? Those things are fattening and full of cholesterol."

"Who's Larimus?" Aunt Hilda asked.

"He was the, uh . . . *pet* . . . that belonged to one of the merchants," Sabrina said.

"Well, if Salem's so intent on giving himself a heart attack, you should've bought more than one bag," Aunt Zelda said.

"Yes," Aunt Hilda added. "Then we wouldn't have to hear Salem whining about them all the time."

"We didn't need to," Salem said. "Sabrina's gonna get me all the Lizard Flakes I want!"

Sabrina's aunts looked at her, and Aunt Zelda asked, "Oh? And how are you going to do that?"

Sabrina smiled as she removed the pleather pouch from the pocket of her sweatshirt. "Well . . . I *did* buy something."

Sabrina's aunts hurried toward her excitedly.

"What is it?" Aunt Zelda asked.

"Let's see!" Aunt Hilda exclaimed.

She handed the pouch to Aunt Hilda and said,

"Open it and look inside." They did. They stared into the pouch for a long moment, frowning.

"You bought glitter?" Aunt Zelda asked.

"No," Sabrina said. "It's wishdust!"

Aunt Zelda and Aunt Hilda lifted their heads, gasped loudly, looked at each other and said simultaneously, *"Wishdust?* Uh-oh!"

"Uh-oh?" Salem blurted.

Sabrina's eyes widened as she asked, "Yeah . . . what do you mean, *uh-oh?* It only cost me seventy-three cents plus tax!"

Sabrina's aunts were still looking at each other, frowning.

"Maybe it's not real," Aunt Zelda said.

"It seems real enough," Sabrina told them. "That's how Salem got his bag of Lizard Flakes. I wished it for him."

"It was the real thing, too," Salem added. "And Sabrina'd never even seen a bag of Lizard Flakes before."

Both aunts sighed heavily and their shoulders sagged.

"I think you should sit down, Sabrina," Aunt Zelda said. "We need to talk." She made a "shoo-shoo" wave at the mountain of merchandise engulfing the kitchen table, and it disappeared in the blink of an eye.

"Iced tea, anyone?" Aunt Hilda asked. She

waved a hand and a tray appeared on the table on which stood a pitcher of tea, with mint and lemons, and three tall glasses.

Sabrina sat down with her aunts, and Salem curled up on the table to listen as they talked.

"First of all," Aunt Zelda said, "the Witch Council took wishdust off the market back in the late fifties because it's always been nothing but trouble."

"You mean it's *illegal?*" Sabrina asked, horrified.

"No, not illegal, nothing like that. It was abolished, simply wiped out by the head of the Witch Council. It's been impossible to find for hundreds of years."

Sabrina cocked her head to the side. "Hundreds of years? I thought it was taken off the market in the fifties."

"That's the *sixteen*-fifties," Aunt Hilda explained.

"Yikes! Well, what kind of trouble was it?" Sabrina asked.

"Wishdust may be pretty, Sabrina," Aunt Zelda said, "and it may sound like a charming thing to have . . . but as the old saying goes, all that glitters is not . . ." She paused, then turned to her sister. "How does that old saying go?"

"I thought it was, all that glows," Aunt Hilda said.

Aunt Zelda frowned. "That wouldn't make

any sense. All that glows is not, what . . . *pluto-nium?* I think it's golden . . . all that glitters is not golden."

"Silence is golden," Sabrina said, rolling her eyes. "All that glitters is not *gold."*

Aunt Zelda and Aunt Hilda turned to give Sabrina a long, blank look.

"What were we talking about?" Aunt Hilda asked.

"Wishdust!" Sabrina and Salem replied impatiently.

Sabrina's aunts took turns speaking as they sweetened their tea.

"Not much is known about wishdust," Aunt Zelda said. "Not anymore, anyway. No one's sure where it came from originally or how it works. Some things are known, though . . . and you may not like them."

"Wishdust can work for anyone, Sabrina . . . anyone," Aunt Hilda added. "In other words, that pouch of wishdust . . ." Aunt Hilda leaned forward and admired the pouch. "Very nice . . . is that real pleather?"

"Yes," Sabrina said with a sigh.

"Well, the wishdust in that pouch will work for anyone who uses it," Aunt Hilda explained. "And I mean anyone."

"But what if it falls into the hands of someone who isn't a witch?" Sabrina asked. "Just a regular mortal?"

"It works for mortals, too," Aunt Hilda said. "I've even heard it works for the dogs on Pluto."

"Only because the dogs on Pluto have opposable thumbs," Aunt Zelda pointed out.

Salem said, "I thought Pluto was a dog."

"Can we please stay on the subject, here?" Sabrina pleaded. "So, let me get this straight. If I were to set this pouch of wishdust down, anybody who picked it up could use it? Even a mortal?"

"It doesn't matter if you set the pouch down," Aunt Zelda said. "Let's say you just spill some of the dust and leave it behind. Someone could come along and pick it up, make a wish, and . . . *voilà!*"

"But wouldn't they have to know how to use it?" Sabrina asked.

"No, that wouldn't matter," Aunt Zelda replied. "Think about it, Sabrina. People wish things all the time . . . secretly . . . in their minds. Let's say someone happened to have some stray wishdust on their fingers and, at the moment they brushed it off, they just happened to make a little wish. Well, then . . ." She shrugged.

Sabrina leaned back in her chair, chewing on her lower lip with worry. "Boy, oh boy," she sighed. "I guess I'd better make sure I don't lose that pouch, then."

Aunt Zelda and Aunt Hilda exchanged a

glance, and Aunt Zelda said, "That's another problem with wishdust. According to everything I've heard, wishdust seems to have a life of its own. The people who possess it have a hard time keeping track of it, because it tends to get lost very easily. Almost like . . . it's trying to get away," she added with a shrug.

Sabrina's eyes grew large. "You mean, it's alive?"

"Not really alive," Aunt Hilda said hesitantly. "Um . . . not exactly. As . . . far as anybody knows."

"Well, that's comforting," Sabrina said with a groan. "Okay . . . let's say I do lose it, or spill some, and someone else finds it and figures out how to use it . . . or just accidentally uses it. And let's say this person manages to do some damage or cause some trouble while using the wishdust. I could fix it, right? I mean, with a spell? With magic?"

Aunt Zelda put her hand on top of Sabrina's hand and said, "That's probably the biggest problem with wishdust, dear. Magic is powerless against anything the wishdust does. Our spells can't reverse its conjurings, no matter how hard we try. That's what worried the Witch Council so much all those centuries ago."

Sabrina put her elbows on the table, her face in her hands, and groaned. "What have I done?"

She turned to Salem. "See? I told you we should've talked to them first!"

"Somehow," Salem muttered, "I knew the blame for this was going to hit me right between the eyes."

Sabrina lifted her head and looked at her aunts. "So . . . what should I do?"

"I'm afraid the wishdust is your responsibility, dear," Aunt Zelda said. "If you want my opinion . . . well, why don't you think it over. If you decide you can handle it, go ahead and keep the dust. If you want, we can go right back to the Rummage Realm and return the wishdust to the person who sold it to you."

"Hey, hey," Salem said, "let's not get too hasty here, okay? We didn't get a receipt. And besides, that old woman might not even have a return policy!"

"You hush," Aunt Zelda whispered to the cat.

"But she said it was her last pouch," Sabrina muttered. "She was going to leave after she sold it."

"Doesn't matter," Aunt Zelda said, shaking her head once. "There's a complete record of every merchant who takes a booth in the Rummage Realm. If she's left, we'll just go find her. But it's up to you."

"Look at it this way, Sabrina," Aunt Hilda said. "Things are a lot different now than they were back in the sixteen-fifties. I mean, maybe you could lock that pouch up in a little safe. Or you could keep it with you all the time and put a lock on your purse, if you'd like."

"Try explaining that at school," Sabrina said with a cold chuckle. "There'd be people trying to break the lock just to see what was in my purse that's important enough to need a lock."

Her aunts exchanged a glance. *Mortals,* they seemed to say with a sigh.

"Well, you know what I mean, don't you?" Aunt Hilda asked.

"Yes, Aunt Hilda," Sabrina said with a smile. "I appreciate the suggestions. I'll give that safe idea some thought. But for now, if you don't mind"—she picked up the pouch and stood up from the table—"I think I'll take my problem upstairs with me. I've got some homework to finish up before tomorrow. As long as I'm up this early . . . I might as well get started."

In her bedroom Sabrina put the pouch of wishdust inside the beautiful music box Harvey had given her. It had been broken once by her cousin Amanda, but Sabrina had put it back together with a little magic. She liked the music box so much, and had been so upset when it was broken, that she even made it unbreakable. So she knew no one would be able to break it open

37

and steal the wishdust. With the wishdust safely tucked away, she changed out of her dusty clothes and put on some comfortable sweats.

Rain pattered against her windowpane, blown by a growing wind. Sabrina loved the rain, and hearing it fall outside always made homework more tolerable. She had an English test to prepare for, and she suspected a quiz in her science class as well, both on Monday. Sabrina opened her book bag and began removing books . . . and she gasped.

"Oh, no!" she cried. "It's not here!" Her English book was not in the bag. She'd left it in her locker. She sat on the edge of her bed with a long, frustrated sigh.

Salem hopped onto the bed beside her and said, "Left a book at school, huh?"

"Yes. And I've got a test."

"Hey, what's the problem? You can just zap it here, can't you?"

"Yeah. I'm just annoyed at myself for leaving the book in my locker." She raised a hand and was about to zap her English book from her locker to bedroom.

"Or," Salem said loudly.

She stopped, looked down at the cat and asked, "Or what?"

"Or . . . you could save your magic and wish the book here with a little dust."

Sabrina frowned. "I don't know. I'm almost

afraid to use that stuff after what Aunt Zelda and
Aunt Hilda said."

"They just want you to be careful not to lose
the pouch, that's all. And you're not likely to lose
it here in your bedroom, are you?"

She thought about it for a while. "No, I guess
not."

"Might as well get your money's worth out of
the stuff, don't you think?"

Finally Sabrina stood, went to her dresser, and
unlocked and opened the music box. She removed the pouch, took out a pinch of wishdust,
and sprinkled it in the air while wishing silently
for her book. The dust sparkled as it fluttered
gracefully to the floor . . . and became Sabrina's
English book. She picked it up and thumbed
through the pages. It was her book, all right . . .
yellow highlights in the right places, doodles in
the corners, and her name written in the front.

"It really does work," Sabrina whispered,
smiling.

"Of course it does!" Salem said happily. "And
now that you've got it out . . . what do you say to
a few more bags of Lizard Flakes?"

Sabrina tossed the book on her bed and said,
"Okay. But then I'm putting it away and no . . .
more . . . wishes, okay?"

"Fine by me . . . as long as you wish up
enough of them."

Sabrina sprinkled some more dust, made another silent wish, and said, "Okay, there."

"Where?" Salem asked, looking around. "I don't see any Lizard Flakes!"

"They're in the pantry. Take your time eating them, okay?"

Salem jumped from the bed and rubbed against Sabrina's leg affectionately. "Oh, Sabrina, you're the best!" He turned and ran out of the room.

Sabrina studied for her English test and brushed up on a few chapters in her science book . . . but it wasn't easy. She kept thinking about the wishdust and everything her aunts had told her.

Her best friend, Val, called to discuss the movie they'd seen last night, the chances of a pop quiz in science, and what Val should wear to her next meeting with the newspaper staff ("I want to look authoritative, but not too authoritative. You know? In charge, but not responsible. Like the principal . . .") But Sabrina was distracted by the music box.

She thought about it all day and into the night. Under normal circumstances, she would have been thinking about the dance coming up at the end of the week and wondering who was going to ask her to it. But it was the wishdust that dominated her thoughts throughout that Sunday. When she finally went to bed, the dust was the last thing on her mind before falling to sleep. . . .

☆

Chapter 5

☆

And it was her first thought upon waking on Monday morning. She thought about it as she quietly ate breakfast, and it was on her mind all the way to school. It remained in the forefront of her thoughts . . . until she saw Mark.

She was heading for her locker when she spotted him down the hall among all the other students, the clatter of locker doors opening and closing, and the din of chatter and laughter. He gave Sabrina his usual shy smile—a smile that made a warm spot blossom in her chest—and she smiled back as they drew closer.

Mark had dark blond hair and deep brown eyes. He was of average height, slender, and had been practically invisible to her until recently because he was so quiet and shy. They'd met one day in the cafeteria when, carrying her tray to a table, Sabrina had been tripped by Cee Cee, one of Libby's cheerleading robot followers. She'd fallen, and her lunch had scattered everywhere as Libby and her friends had a good laugh over the spectacle.

"Are you all right?" a quiet voice had asked.

Looking up, Sabrina had seen Mark hunkering down beside her, smiling. He'd helped her gather the spilled lunch back onto the tray. After returning it, he'd gone through the line with her for another lunch. Mark said he'd seen Cee Cee trip her, and Sabrina said she wasn't surprised. They had a few laughs about Libby and her friends—"You mean, the bimbots?" Mark had asked—and they'd ended up eating lunch together and talking.

Sabrina had wondered that day how it was she hadn't noticed Mark until then. He was very good-looking in a gentle sort of way, soft-spoken but very funny . . . and he was so nice. Part of the reason was that she'd been focusing all her attention on Harvey. Now that their relationship was on hold, she'd been seeing other guys . . . and she'd noticed Mark. As they'd gotten to know each other over the last two weeks, Mark had, in his own quiet and unassuming way, treated Sabrina like a queen.

"How was your weekend, Mark?" Sabrina asked as they met in the hall. They were a tiny island in the river of students flowing around them.

"Pretty boring, I guess," he said. "My great-aunt Marsha's visiting, and she's pretty strict. I just hung out, played on the computer, did some homework. You think we're going to have that quiz in science class today?"

"I studied for it, just in case."

"Me, too." He smiled again, looked down at his feet and cleared his throat. "You know, uh . . . I'd kind of like to . . . well, I'd like to talk to you, Sabrina. Do you think maybe, um . . . well, could have lunch together today?"

"Sure!" Sabrina exclaimed, sounding more excited than she'd intended.

Mark's smile became a grin, and he exhaled a great breath, as if in relief. "Let me get my books, and I'll meet you at your locker."

Sabrina went to her locker and ran into Valerie.

"He really is cute, y'know?" Valerie said. She followed Sabrina to her locker. "I mean, who'd have thought we could miss somebody who's so cute? You know what I mean?"

Sabrina chuckled and nodded as she opened her locker. "I know what you mean, Valerie."

"Hey . . . did you hear they're making a movie right here in town?"

Sabrina's eyebrows popped up as she turned to her friend. "No, I hadn't heard."

"Yeah, and guess who's starring? Winona Ryder and . . . are you ready for this? Brad Pitt!"

"Are you serious?" Sabrina asked, wide-eyed. "I haven't heard anything about this!"

"Well, that's the rumor," Valerie said with a shrug.

Sabrina rolled her eyes with a smile. "Ah, a rumor." Val loved rumors almost as much as she loved gossip. Anything that made her interesting to other people.

Sabrina kept the books for her first two classes, left her purse hanging from her shoulder, and slammed her locker.

"You're keeping your purse?" Valerie asked.

"Yes, I am."

"Don't you usually put it in your locker?"

"Well . . . today I just feel like keeping it with me."

"Got something important in there?" Valerie asked with a smirk.

"Not really. Just the usual stuff."

"Then why are you carrying it with you today?"

"Because it goes with my oufit," Sabrina said with a smile.

Valerie looked at Sabrina's little black purse with red stitching, then looked at her red georgette shirt over a black T-shirt and pants. "Yeah . . . you're right, it does go with your sweater! Good call, Sabrina!" Valerie smiled,

44

said she had to get her stuff and head for her first class, then disappeared into the crowded hall.

Sabrina's purse did not hold the usual stuff, of course. It held the pleather pouch of wishdust. The pouch was zipped up in a small pocket inside the purse, and there it would remain until she went home and could lock it in the music box again. She'd decided that morning to keep the wishdust with her at all times. After what her aunts had told her, Sabrina was taking no chances.

"Let me carry your books," Mark said from behind her.

Sabrina turned to him with a grin, handed over her books, and they made their way to her homeroom.

For the first half of the day, the wishdust Sabrina carried in her purse was completely forgotten. She could wonder only about her lunch with Mark . . . and whether or not he would ask her to the dance.

The upcoming dance was celebrating no holiday, and it certainly wasn't a prom. It was, in fact, just another dance. Libby was well on her way to having at least one dance a month. The dance committee was made up of the usual suspects: Libby and her friends. But when one of those girls contracted mono, there was an opening to be filled. Ms. O'Connor, the home economics teacher and one of the Student Council advisors, suggested that the opening be filled by someone who had never worked on a dance committee before. She suggested Valerie . . . and she did so firmly. As much as Libby hated to do it, she had to accept Valerie as a member of the committee.

Valerie, of course, had been so flabbergasted by her position on the committee that she'd collapsed into a fit of stammering and stuttering and bobbing up and down as if she were dodging bullets. When she'd finally accepted the fact that she was a member of the planning committee, she saved the stuttering, stammering, and bobbing for the people she *told* she was a member of the committee . . . people like Sabrina.

Knowing how shy Mark was—even after two weeks of talking and spending time together—Sabrina wondered if he would be able to muster the courage to ask her to the dance. If so, she hoped he would do it soon. She would happily turn all others down in favor of Mark (except Harvey, but he was playing the field as his parents wanted) . . . but what if she did that, and then he didn't ask her? Sabrina decided if it came to that, *she* would ask *him* to the dance!

She suspected that wouldn't be necessary, though. When they'd talked that morning and he'd asked to have lunch with her, he'd sounded so nervous, as if he'd had something on his mind. Sabrina was hoping that maybe . . . just maybe . . . he had the dance on his mind and was planning to ask her to be his date.

When the lunch bell rang, Sabrina couldn't get to her locker fast enough. She hurried down the hall, rounded the corner . . . and then chaos broke out.

There was never a definite explanation for the riotous behavior of the students, but Sabrina didn't need one. She kept hearing two names uttered as the oceanlike wave of students poured through the hall: "Brad Pitt" and "Winona Ryder." That was all the explanation she needed. Students were falling over one another to get to the front of the building . . . and Sabrina was in the way. She was knocked to the floor, and her purse fell loose from her shoulder.

As the stampede passed, Sabrina's purse was kicked in all directions by running feet. It shot like a pinball from once side of the hall to the other, moving forward all the while, out of her reach.

"No!" Sabrina cried, stumbling to her feet. She pressed herself against the lockers for a moment, to let the others pass. As soon as the foot traffic thinned, she hurried down the hall to find her purse.

But she couldn't find it! She went all the way to the main entrance and found bits and pieces of the contents of her purse—a comb here, a lipstick there—but she still couldn't find the purse. She looked out the glass doors and saw the mass of students gathered outside, then stepped out the doors to see what they were looking at.

Across the street, a utility truck was parked at the curb. Suspended high above the truck was a man in a basket, working on one of the power poles.

Sabrina looked over the crowd of students. They were quiet, looking around desperately, murmuring their disappointment.

Sabrina put her hands on her hips and called out, "I heard Brad Pitt and Winona Ryder are having lunch down at the Grub Stop Diner!"

Suddenly the crowd of students roared and rushed down the front steps, turned right, and ran down the sidewalk. They were like a swarm of bees sent on a mission by their queen.

Sabrina rolled her eyes, turned to go back inside . . . and spotted her purse. It was crumpled in the corner outside the doors of the school, clasp open, strap tattered, black satin scuffed. She picked it up and went back inside, then stopped to inspect the purse. Inside, the compartment holding the pouch of wishdust was still tightly zipped shut. The pouch was safe.

She patted a hand over her hair and realized she was a mess after being knocked around by the stampede of star-crazed students. Sabrina decided to go to the restroom and straighten herself out. She didn't want to look like roadkill for her lunch with Mark.

Sabrina did not realize, as she rushed toward the restroom, that her purse had been so abused that a number of small holes had been opened in the side. Nor did she realize that while the purse was being kicked down the hall and bouncing off the walls, the pouch of wishdust had opened up inside . . . not completely, but just enough to spill some of the glittery dust it held. . . .

"There you are," Valerie said when Sabrina walked into the restroom. Valerie was standing at the end of the counter facing the mirror, running a brush through her hair. There were several other girls there, too, all lined up along the counter, putting on makeup and brushing their hair. Valerie's mouth dropped open as she looked at Sabrina. "Wow, you look like you were hit by a bus!"

Sabrina went to Valerie's side and put her purse on the end of the counter. "Not a bus," she said. "Just a bunch of students who thought they were going to see Brad Pitt and Winona Ryder."

Valerie's eyes grew wide. "They're here?"

"No, no. Just a utility truck across the street. Apparently somebody thought it was for the movie, and there was a stampede." She looked at her hands and winced. "I'm filthy, and I'm supposed to have lunch with Mark. I think he's going to ask me to the dance!"

"Then pull yourself together, girl!"

"Be right back," Sabrina said. She walked behind the line of girls before the mirror, went to a sink, and washed her face and hands. Once she'd dried, she stepped in front of the mirror and made a noise of disgust in her throat. She leaned forwered and looked down the line of girls toward Valerie, who had a compact open in front of her at the other end. "Hey, Valerie! Could you pass my purse down?"

At the opposite end of the counter, Valerie picked up Sabrina's purse.

Inside, the slightly opened bag of wishdust tilted in its zippered compartment. The sparkling dust began to spill from the bag. After being kicked around in the hall earlier, the purse was riddled with tiny holes and tears . . . and some of them were on the outside of the zippered compartment holding the pleather pouch.

Valerie passed Sabrina's purse to the girl to her left . . . and as she did, some of the dust trickled from the tiny holes in the side of the purse and fell silently and unnoticed into Valerie's compact. As the purse was passed down the line, the wishdust continued to seep from the purse, falling into compacts, into hands and hair-brushes . . . until it was handed to Sabrina.

"I'm a mess," she muttered, looking at herself in the mirror. She opened her purse, removed her brush, and began running it through her hair, oblivious to what had just happened.

Chapter 6

☆

They're serving the macaroni and cheese in blocks today," Sabrina said as she sat down across from Mark with her lunch tray.

"Yeah," he said with a quiet chuckle. "I was thinking of saving mine."

"Really? Why?"

"Well, I don't know." He shrugged, smirked at her. "I thought it might come in handy for some science project down the line."

Sabrina laughed. "So, Mark, how's your day gone so far?"

"Not bad. But I haven't seen Winona Ryder or Brad Pitt yet."

"Don't hold your breath. I don't know where that rumor came from, but I think it's a bunch of . . . well, a bunch of macaroni and cheese."

They talked as they ate, but the conversation

never made its way to the dance. Sabrina began to wonder if she'd misread Mark that morning. Maybe he'd just seemed nervous because . . . he was nervous. She decided to poke around a little.

"What are you doing this weekend, Mark? Do you have any plans?"

Mark dropped his fork in his root beer. "Uh, this wuh-weekend? Or, um . . . do you mean this weekend?"

Sabrina swallowed a laugh. "I mean the weekend that starts after school this coming Friday."

"Oh. Oh. You mean . . . that weekend. Well . . . I was thinking, you know . . . actually, I was hoping, Sabrina . . ."

When he didn't go on, Sabrina pressed him. "Yes? You were hoping . . . what?"

"Well, I was hoping that maybe we could—"

There was a clatter as a lunch tray was dropped onto the table beside Sabrina.

"Hey, you two," Valerie said, dropping into a chair. "Have you heard that Brad Pitt and Winona Ryder are having lunch down at the Grub Stop Diner? I mean . . . they're having lunch there right now!"

Mark fell silent, leaned forward, and began eating his lunch.

Sabrina closed her eyes and sighed.

"Um, don't you guys care?" Valerie asked. "I mean, they're just down the street from us right now!"

"I started that rumor, Valerie," Sabrina said, turning to Valerie.

"What? You started . . . but why? Why would you do something like that?"

"Because I could, Valerie. Anybody can. All you have to do is say something like that and everybody believes you. They're like lemmings . . . all you have to do is point and say, 'There's the cliff!' Besides . . . I said Brad Pitt and Winona Ryder were at the diner because all those nimrods had just nearly killed me in the hall." Sabrina frowned slightly as she looked at her friend. There was something different about Valerie's face . . . something vaguely different . . . but Sabrina couldn't put a finger on it.

"Oh. Well." Valerie frowned for a moment. "I guess that's pretty profound. Doesn't say a whole lot for rumors, I suppose . . . does it, Sabrina?"

"Nope, it doesn't," Sabrina said, still looking at Valerie, trying to figure out what was different about her face. She finally gave up. "So, uh . . . just ignore that stuff about the movie and the movie stars, okay?"

"Hey, guys," Harvey said as he sat down at the end of the table with his lunch tray.

Sabrina tried not to let her frustration show on her face. She'd suspected Mark would be reluctant to ask her to the dance if Valerie was listening in. With Harvey at the table, there wasn't a chance. Mark was just too shy.

"Did you hear Neve Campbell and Leonardo DiCaprio are making a movie in town?" Harvey asked.

"Brad Pitt and Winona Ryder," Valerie corrected him.

"Except it's all a rumor and there are no movie stars and no movie," Sabrina said.

"That's too bad," Harvey said with a frown. "I was hoping to get an autograph. I really like Neve Campbell. Or . . . um, Winona Ryder. Whoever."

There was a moment of silence among the four of them as they ate their lunch.

"Hey, Mark," Valerie said, "have you asked Sab—"

Sabrina burst into a coughing fit and pounded a hand on the tabletop to shut Valerie up.

Valerie turned and put a hand on Sabrina's back. "Are you okay? You all right, Sabrina?"

"Want me to get you some water?" Harvey asked.

"Fine, fine . . . I'm fine."

"Are you sure?" Mark asked as he reached across the table and put a hand over hers.

Sabrina froze . . . and smiled across the table at Mark. "Yes," she said. "I'm sure."

There was a sudden commotion on the other side of the cafeteria. Voices rose and several tables emptied in an instant as people rushed toward the door.

"Another rumor, maybe," Valerie said.

"Probably another stampede," Sabrina said. "They probably think they're going to see—"

The unmistakable roaring trumpet of an elephant sounded outside the cafeteria.

Sabrina, Mark, Valerie, and Harvey froze and exchanged surprised looks.

After a long moment Harvey said, "I don't know about you guys, but that, um . . . that sounded to me like an eleph—"

The trumpeting sound came again, followed by a loud cheer from a mass of voices.

Sabrina felt a flutter in her chest, a tiny bit of panic. "Okay," she said, putting her purse strap over her shoulder again, "let's go see what's going on."

They left their lunches, made their way across the cafeteria to the door, and stepped through. All four of them gasped loudly.

An elephant stood in the hall, surrounded by gaping students.

"A new student, you think?" Valerie asked.

Sabrina shook her head. "Not unless they've made some killer changes in the curriculum."

"Is there a circus in town?" Mark asked.

"I don't know," Harvey said. "But if they don't get that thing out of here soon, the janitor's gonna be ticked."

Sabrina could hardly contain the sudden fear that clogged her throat. "S'cuse me," she said as she stepped away from her friends and opened her purse. The zipper on the interior compartment was completely, firmly closed, which relieved her somewhat. When she opened the zipper, she found the pouch in place, which made her feel even better. But some of the wishdust had spilled from it and was puddled in the corner of the compartment.

Okay, Sabrina thought frantically, *so some of it spilled. It spilled inside my purse. That couldn't possibly account for an elephant in the hall outside the cafeteria.*

She turned back to her friends and asked Valerie, "Remember when I came into the restroom a little earlier and left my purse next to you while I went to the sink and washed up?"

"Yeah," Valerie said with a nod.

"Well, did you or anyone else open my purse and get into it?"

Valerie's face screwed into an expression of painful disappointment. "Sabrina! I can't believe you'd accuse me of doing something like—"

"I'm not accusing you, Valerie, I'm just wondering, that's all. I mean, if you did"—Sabrina tried to smile sincerely—"it's okay. I'm just wondering."

"No, I didn't. And neither did anyone else. It was right there the whole time and nobody touched it until I passed it down to you."

Valerie turned away from her and stared, like

everyone else, at the monstrous but docile elephant.

Sabrina felt a tapping on her shoulder and turned to see Mr. Kraft. He was smiling down at her with his usual sickly-sweet, completely insincere smile. He stood with his hands joined behind him as he rocked on his heels. "Tell me something, Miss Spellman," the vice-principal said, still smiling. "You wouldn't happen to know how an elephant came to be standing in the hall of Westbridge High at lunchtime?"

"What makes you think I would know, Mr. Kraft?" Sabrina asked. "I mean, none of these people seems to know. I don't know if anybody knows."

"Oh, I'm sure someone knows, Miss Spellman. Someone, somewhere."

The elephant turned its head toward Mr. Kraft and slowly reached out with its trunk.

"But for the time being," Mr. Kraft continued, "I'm asking you, Miss Spellman. And so far, you have not answered my question. So I'll ask again. Do you, or do you not, know why there's an——"

The elephant wrapped the end of its trunk around Mr. Kraft's tie and tugged.

Mr. Kraft made an "ack" sound as he stumbled forward, then looked up at the elephant and tried to smile. He couldn't even manage an insincere upturning of his mouth. He reached up

and patted the elephant's trunk carefully.
"Down, boy. Guh-good, boy."

The elephant tugged on Mr. Kraft's tie again,
harder this time, making him stumble forward
even more clumsily.

"Hey," Mr. Kraft called. "Hey! Somebody
give me a hand here!"

Sabrina started to laugh in spite of the situation but held it back. Then Valerie and Mark
and Harvey started to laugh, too . . . but they
didn't hold it back.

"This is not funny!" Mr. Kraft snapped at
them.

Others in the crowd of onlookers began laughing as well, until everyone was laughing at Mr.
Kraft.

The elephant tugged harder on the tie, pulling
Mr. Kraft closer and closer.

"Listen to me," Mr. Kraft said desperately,
looking up at the elephant, "this is my first year
at this school. I wasn't prepared for this kind of
situation!"

It wasn't long before Mrs. Juarez, the principal's secretary, and Mr. Grotch, the football
coach, hurried to Mr. Kraft's rescue. As they
were trying to pry the elephant's trunk from Mr.
Kraft's tie, other school officials and some police
officers arrived to herd the elephant outside. The
crowd began to disperse. Everyone went back

into the cafeteria to finish lunch before the period ended, including Sabrina and her friends.

On the way back to their table, Sabrina heard her friends talking, but they sounded distant. She was too busy trying to figure out how the wishdust might be attached to the sudden appearance of an elephant in the hall. But no matter how hard she tried, she couldn't put the two together. It just didn't make sense that her wishdust could have something to do with that elephant, no matter how bizarre its appearance might be.

"Hey, maybe that elephant's part of the movie," Harvey said as they took their seats at the table. "I mean, you know, maybe Neve Campbell and Brad Pitt are doing a movie about an elephant."

"Brad Pitt and Winona Ryder," Valerie corrected him.

"Whoever."

"Except there's no movie because the whole thing's a rumor," Valerie added. "Right, Sabrina?"

Sabrina was shaken from her thoughts by the question. "A rumor? Well . . . who knows, right?"

Valerie frowned. "But I thought you said it was a rumor."

"I did, but . . . how else do you explain the

elephant?" Sabrina smiled and continued eating her lunch.

I hope *it's not a rumor,* Sabrina thought. *Because if it is, then I've missed something . . . and something's really wrong.*

Outside the cafeteria, they heard the elephant trumpet again.

"Did you have to cut it?" Mr. Kraft shouted beyond the door. "Thuh-that was an original Jerry Garcia, for crying out loud! Do you know how much that tie cost?"

Sabrina looked around at her friends and saw them smiling. A moment later, all four of them were laughing hysterically.

☆

Chapter 7

☆

The rest of the day seemed endless to Sabrina. She was so preoccupied with the elephant and its possible link to her wishdust that she found it difficult to pay attention in her classes. She performed terribly on her English test, finished early, and left the class. She walked down the hall with a frown darkening her face, lost in thought, and almost ran into Mr. Kraft.

The vice-principal's blond hair was mussed, his shoulders were drooping, his glasses were crooked, and his eyes were wide and staring. He was still wearing what was left of his original Jerry Garcia tie . . . which was a little over two inches that came to an abrupt end where someone had snipped the rest of the tie off with a pair of scissors.

When he saw Sabrina, Mr. Kraft quickly

straightened his posture. He reached up and ran a hand through his hair, straightened his glasses, and tried to smile. "Well, Miss Spellman. What brings you into the hall during fifth period?"

"We had an English test and I finished a little early."

"How nice for you. And where are you headed?"

"To the restroom."

"Well, I hope it can wait. I'm on my way to, uh . . . well, I'm, uh, going to my, uh . . . office." He coughed, fidgeted a little. "I'd like you to come with me. I want to have a word with you."

Sabrina sighed. "Look, Mr. Kraft, if it's about that elephant—"

"We'll talk about it in my office." He didn't move. Just stood there. "Shall we go?"

"Sure," Sabrina said.

"Well, uh . . . go ahead. You lead the way, Miss Spellman."

Uh-oh, Sabrina thought. *Something's not right here. There's something very weird about Mr. Kraft . . . something even weirder than usual.*

Sabrina started to walk, but turned her head to keep an eye on Mr. Kraft. He walked a half-step behind her as they turned left and went down another hall.

"How did your English test go, Miss Spellman?"

"Terribly."

"You should study more."

"I studied a lot."

"Then you should study even more."

She looked at his tie again and tried to keep from laughing. "Sorry about your tie, Mr. Kraft."

He made a grumbling sound in his throat. "A Jerry Garcia original," he muttered, shaking his head. "You probably don't know who Jerry Garcia was, do you? Of course you don't."

"I know who he was," Sabrina said defensively. "The Grateful Dead."

"Ah. You surprise me, Miss Spellman. I thought your generation knew nothing beyond the Spice Girls and Marilyn Manson."

"Marilyn who?" she asked with the slightest of smirks.

They rounded another corner, with Mr. Kraft walking beside Sabrina instead of a bit behind her.

"I saw the Grateful Dead perform live. I saw them at Woodstock." He glanced at her as he fondled what remained of his Jerry Garcia tie. "Are you familiar with Woodstock, Miss Spellman?"

Sabrina knew that Woodstock was a weekend-long rock concert that took place in upstate New York in the late sixties, but she wanted to annoy Mr. Kraft. "Isn't that the little bird that hangs out with Snoopy in the *Peanuts* comic strip?"

They turned right, and Sabrina became concerned. They were nowhere near Mr. Kraft's office, and they were going even farther in the wrong direction.

Mr. Kraft rolled his eyes, threw up his arms and let them slap to his sides. "You see? You see? Just when you were starting to impress me, Miss Spellman." He shook his head and sighed. "But I don't know why I'm surprised. Young people today have no respect for the past or for their elders. Do you know that not ten minutes ago, a student said to me—some girl, I don't know her name, but I'm going to find out—she said, 'I wish you'd get lost.' Can you believe that? A student telling the vice-principal to get lost!"

Sabrina winced. "Well, Mr. Kraft, um . . . I was about to bring up that very subject."

"What? What are you talking about?"

"I thought you said you wanted to go to your office."

"Yes, that's right."

"Well, your office is on the other side of the building."

He stopped walking and turned to her excitedly. "It is? Where?"

"Don't you know where your office is?"

Mr. Kraft suddenly looked very serious. He leaned close to her and lowered his voice to a near whisper. "There is something very bizarre going on at Westbridge High today, Miss Spellman. First, an elephant appears outside the cafeteria . . . out of nowhere. Then . . . and then . . . a student says she wishes I'd get lost, and . . . and I do. I haven't been able to find my office. I've looked everywhere, but I can't find it, and I'm not sure I'd recognize it if I did. I was hoping you would lead me to it so we could have a little talk, but that didn't work. So I suggest we talk here and now. What . . . is going on . . . Miss Spellman?"

Sabrina felt panic begin to burst inside her again and again, like fireworks. Someone had wished Mr. Kraft would get lost . . . and he did. There was no mistaking that, not even if she tried. It was definitely the work of wishdust. She started to speak, but Mr. Kraft interrupted her, holding up a stiff forefinger.

"Don't try to deny it. You've been responsible for some very odd things, Miss Spellman. I'm not sure which odd things, and I have no proof of any of it, but I know it, and so do you. So tell me what's going on here today!"

Sabrina thought fast. She had to calm him down so she could find out which student had wanted him to get lost. She gave him a puzzled stare, cocked her head, and asked, "Are you sure you're feeling okay, Mr. Kraft? I mean . . . do you hear what you're saying? First you tell me you can't find your office, and then you think I'm responsible for that and an elephant in the hallway? Would you like me to get someone? One of the teachers? The principal, maybe?"

He didn't move for a long moment, didn't even blink, just stared at her with wide eyes and a pointing finger.

"I can take you there, if you'd like," she continued in a low, soothing voice. "I'm sure no one would want you working while you're feeling this . . . confused."

He still did not move.

"Um . . . Mr. Kraft?"

Suddenly his finger folded inward and he stood up straight. He patted his hair, cleared his throat, and straightened his tie as if it were all there. "You're exactly right, Miss Spellman. I should, uh . . . yes, I suppose I should see the nurse. And no thank you, I can find the nurse's office myself. I said I couldn't find my office; I didn't say anything about the nurse's office."

"Uh, Mr. Kraft . . . about that student . . . the one who said she wished you'd get lost. You don't know who she is?"

"No. But I was going to find out in my office."

"Well, I wouldn't mind knowing myself. If you'd like, I really will take you to your office. When you're done, you can go see the nurse and—"

The bell rang and classrooms suddenly began to empty.

"I appreciate your offer, Miss Spellman," Mr.

Kraft said with another smarmy smile, "but frankly . . . you frighten me. And it just occurred to me that there is a map of this building on the wall in the nurse's office. I can use that to find my office after I . . . well, get a couple aspirins, or something. But I'll be wanting to speak with you later, Miss Spellman."

The hall was growing crowded around them as students hurried to their lockers.

"Really? Would you like me to come to your office? What time? I'll be happy to come in after my last class."

He chuckled. "You seem awfully eager."

"Well, I want to, um . . . you know . . . cooperate."

"Fine. Come in after your last class. I won't keep you long . . . but I intend to get to the bottom of things."

Sabrina nodded and turned to leave.

"Uh . . . one more thing, Miss Spellman," Mr. Kraft said. "Do you think you could, um . . . well, perhaps you could point me in the direction of the nurse's office."

Sabrina smiled and pointed behind him. "Straight down the hall and turn left at the drinking fountains. It's the second door on your left."

Mr. Kraft still looked a bit confused as he turned around and headed down the hall. He walked unsteadily for a few seconds, then with a stiff spine, a sure step, and his head held high in his usual haughty way.

Sabrina went to her locker, got the book she needed, and turned to head for class. Valerie was approaching her, and they almost collided.

"Does this day stink, or what?" Valerie asked as they began to walk to class together. "First, we have the English test from Mars . . . and after this period, we're going to have a quiz in science. I'd rather hang out with the elephant, to tell you the truth."

Sabrina looked at Valerie and thought, once again, that there was something different about her face . . . she just couldn't put her finger on it.

"Have you changed your hair, Valerie?" Sabrina asked.

"No. Why?"

"Well . . . I'm just wondering. Are you, um . . . wearing different makeup, or something?"

"No. Why? Do I look weird?" Valerie's voice rose in panic.

"Not weird, just . . . different. I just can't figure out—"

Sabrina was interrupted when Mark joined them and said, "Hey, you two. How'd you do on the English test?"

"My head hurts so much from the test," Valerie said, "I don't even know."

Sabrina said, "I did badly, I think. I mean, I

did my best, but . . . I don't think that was very good."

Mark placed a hand on her arm gently and said, "It's just one test. It's not the end of the world."

The spot on Sabrina's arm where Mark was touching her felt warm . . . and that warmth spread. She smiled at him, moved closer to him, and put an arm around his waist. "Thanks, Mark," she said.

"Hey," he said, "you think we can get together right after school? I could even drive you home, if you'd like. I'd just like to, um . . . well, you know . . . we still haven't talked."

Sabrina's eyes brightened for a moment, and she started to agree . . . but then she remembered her meeting with Mr. Kraft. "I'm sorry. I have to meet with the vice-principal right after school."

"Okay," Mark said. "I can wait for you."

"Are you serious?"

"Sure, I'm serious. I'll wait for you, and when you're done I can take you home. And somewhere in between, we can talk." He smiled at her.

"Really? Okay. If you'll wait for me, you've got a deal." She returned his smile.

In the classroom, they took their seats.

Valerie, who sat in the seat to Sabrina's right, turned to Sabrina and said, "Don't you just wish this day would end? I mean, I don't know about you, but it's been a lousy day for me. It really stinks, this day does."

Sabrina turned to her friend and said, "Yeah, it's been a pretty weird day for me, too." But she couldn't turn away. There really was something different about Valerie's face. "Hey, Val . . . you're doing something different, aren't you? With your hair, maybe?"

"My hair? No . . . nothing different. Why?"

"Different makeup?"

"Same makeup I've always used. Why? What's the matter? Do I look like a dork, or something?"

"No, no, it's just that . . ." Sabrina suddenly realized what was different about Valerie's face. It was sparkling!

Uh-oh!

Sabrina felt a jolt of fear in her chest, as if someone had just dumped a bucket of ice cubes on her. She put her purse on her lap, reached inside, and pulled the zipper open. The pouch was still in its compartment.

"Valerie, you're sparkling," Sabrina said. "Around your eyes. You've got little sparkling things around your eyes!"

"Oh, that's probably from working on the dance decorations. They're using a lot of glitter." Valerie sighed, reached up and swept a hand over one cheek, then the other. She looked at her

71

hand and said, "Yeah, glitter." She held her hand out and brushed her fingers together, sending sparkling bits into the air.

"No, no, don't—" Sabrina began, but Valerie interrupted her.

"I don't know about you, but I wish this school day would just end so we could all go home."

Half a second later, the overhead sprinkler system, designed to activate when there was a fire in the building, went off. It began to rain on everyone in the room, as if they were sitting outside in a storm.

Sabrina yelped as the sprinklers soaked her and everyone else. A few screams rose from girls in the classroom, and a couple guys shouted angrily. Desks were knocked over as students shot to their feet and rushed for the door.

Clutching her purse, Sabrina got up and started out of the room with Valerie. The wet floor was slippery, and a couple people stumbled at the door, falling out of the room. Sabrina was about five feet from the door when her feet slipped out from under her, and she fell backward, landing hard on her behind.

Her purse flew from her grip and tumbled through the air, spilling its contents on the way across the room. The purse landed somewhere with a wet slap . . . and everything that had been in the purse landed everywhere else.

"What are you doing?" Valerie asked as Sabrina got to her feet and walked back toward the desks.

"I lost my purse!" Sabrina replied, shouting to be heard above the downpour.

"Okay," Valerie said. "See you outside!" She hurried out the door.

Sabrina was the only person left in the room . . . and she was drenched. Moving quickly, she picked up her purse, then hunched down and walked in a crouch as she plucked her belongings from the wet floor. When she thought she'd retrieved the last one, she looked in her purse.

The zipper was open and the pouch was gone. She'd had the compartment unzipped when the sprinklers went off . . . and the pouch had flown out with everything else when the purse flew through the air.

Sabrina's chest tightened with panic as she scanned the floor for the pleather pouch. When she didn't see it, she got on her hands and knees and looked under desks and bookshelves. She covered every inch of the floor as the sprinklers continued to spray water everywhere.

The pouch of wishdust was nowhere to be found . . . but Sabrina spotted an unmistakable iridescent glimmer in the water on the floor. She reached down and scooped it up on her fingertips. It was wishdust, all right . . . there was no mistaking it. But it wasn't all of the wishdust, just a tiny bit.

An idea came to her and brightened her eyes, made her tense muscles relax a little. She rubbed the pad of her thumb over her fingertips and tried to sprinkle the wishdust. At the same time, she closed her eyes and thought, *I wish I could find my pouch of wishdust.* She opened her eyes and looked around.

The pouch was nowhere in sight.

Sabrina looked down at the tiny bits of glimmering wishdust. It hadn't worked! She bent down, scooped it up on her fingertips again as the water continued to rain from above. She tried to sprinkle it a second time, but it wouldn't sprinkle. It just dropped to the floor in a tiny, soggy clump.

Clearly the wishdust didn't work if it was wet. *Great!* Now *I find this out!*

For the time being, the information was useless . . . because the wishdust was no longer in her possession . . . and Sabrina had no idea where it had gone.

☆

Chapter 8

☆

When Sabrina got home, she entered the house silently wearing soaking wet clothes. She didn't want to be heard because she didn't want to talk to anyone. She simply wasn't ready to tell her aunts that she'd lost the wishdust—

"Sabrina?" Aunt Zelda called. "Is that you?"

Sabrina sighed and closed her eyes. Where her aunts were concerned, there was no such thing as entering the house silently. She'd planned to go upstairs and take a hot shower before putting on some dry clothes, but instead, she waved her hand. Her clothes were perfectly dry in an instant. She wondered why she hadn't done that sooner.

"Yes, Aunt Zelda."

Sabrina stepped into the living room and looked around. Aunt Zelda's voice had come from the living room, but she was nowhere to be seen.

"Aunt Zelda?" Sabrina called.

"Up here, dear."

Sabrina looked up and around. Aunt Zelda was hovering high above the floor with her nose in a corner of the living room.

Sabrina frowned and asked, "What are you doing up there?"

"Oh," Aunt Zelda said with a sigh, "just . . . thinking about what I might fix for dinner tonight . . . if I get down from here by then."

Sabrina's eyes suddenly brightened. Aunt Zelda hovering in the corner could only mean one thing.

"Is Great-Grandma here?" Sabrina asked.

"Yes. How did you know?"

"Well, the only other time Great-Grandma came here, you ended up floating in the corner," Sabrina said with a smirk. She was happy to hear Great-Grandma was around because, with her years of wisdom, she just might be able to help Sabrina with her wishdust problem.

"What's she doing here?" Sabrina asked.

"She just dropped in to visit and give us a batch of her yogurt and parsley fudge."

"What did you do this time, Aunt Zelda?"

"I didn't do anything! I just happened to mention, in passing, how often I use my Lab-

Top. She thinks that shows laziness and a lack of resourcefulness in a witch, so . . . here I am."

"Where is Great-Grandma now?" Sabrina asked.

"In the kitchen exchanging spell recipes with Hilda. She always liked Hilda more than me." Aunt Zelda folded her arms in front of her and huffed indignantly.

Sabrina went into the kitchen and found Aunt Hilda at the island, hunched over a notebook and writing furiously as Great-Grandma spoke.

". . . but the rat tails," Great-Grandma was saying in her slightly shaky voice, "must be completely plucked of all hairs, no matter how fine." She turned around and grinned. "Sabrina! How good to see you!"

"Hello, Great-Grandma," Sabrina said. She put her book bag on the table, went to the old woman, and gave her a big hug.

"How was your day, Sabrina?" Aunt Hilda asked.

"Oh, well, it was, um . . . it was . . . interesting."

"That's good," Aunt Hilda said, smiling.

Great-Grandma frowned and put a hand on Sabrina's shoulder. "Something's wrong. Something bad happened to you today, didn't it, dear?"

"Well, yes . . . something bad did happen," Sabrina said.

"Oh, well, I knew that," Aunt Hilda said. "I was just trying to be positive about things . . . y'know?"

"What happened?" Great-Grandma asked.

"Um, do you think maybe I can get the rest of this spell recipe?" Aunt Hilda asked.

Great-Grandma turned to her and said, "A little later, Hilda. This young lady's problems come first." She turned to Sabrina again and said, "Tell me."

"It's kind of a long story," Sabrina said reluctantly.

"In that case, I'll need some tea." Great-Grandma lifted her hand, palm up, and in it appeared a cup of steaming tea on a saucer. "Shall we go in the living room and get comfortable?"

Sabrina nodded and they left the kitchen. Aunt Hilda followed, somewhat bewildered.

Great-Grandma and Aunt Hilda seated themselves on the sofa. Sabrina was too jittery to sit. She remained standing as she began telling Great-Grandma her story. She was on her third sentence when Aunt Zelda called from above.

"Can I come down now, Great-Grandma?"

"Hush up, Zelda," Great-Grandma said with an upward glance over her shoulder. "I still haven't decided how long you should be up there. If you're lazy enough to use a Lab-Top, then you must enjoy doing nothing . . . so you can just stay up there doing nothing for a while longer." She turned to Sabrina again, smiled, and said, "Go on, dear."

Sabrina continued her story. At the mention of wishdust, Great-Grandma's jaw dropped, her eyes bulged, and she took in a long, deep gasp.

"Wishdust?" Great-Grandma said with shock. "Where did you get wishdust? What kind of neighborhoods have you been visiting?" She looked over her shoulder and upward. "Zelda, in what kind of neighborhoods have you been letting Sabrina hang out?"

When Sabrina told Great-Grandma she'd gotten the wishdust in the Rummage Realm, the old woman became even more upset.

"Is this true, Hilda?" Great-Grandma asked. "Did you take Sabrina to the Rummage Realm and let her wander around on her own? In that dump? In that den of thieves?"

Aunt Hilda became wary. "Well, she just left us to get something to eat with Salem, that's all!"

"A *cat?* You left her in the company of a cat? That's *all?* She would have been safer alone at a convention of—" Great-Grandma took a deep breath and let it out slowly. "As a result of your negligence, she bought a pouch of wishdust. Wishdust! You should be ashamed of yourselves for letting your niece run off on her own in that kind of environment!"

Aunt Hilda looked horrified. Her wide eyes

looked ready to pop out, and her mouth worked frantically, trying to find the right thing to say. She glanced, now and then, at her sister hovering in the corner as a result of Great-Grandma's disapproval. "Buh-but we just wanted to show her the realm, that's all!"

Great-Grandma turned to Sabrina again and said, "Listen to me, dear. That wishdust will be nothing but trouble for you. It's very important that you give it to me so I can see that it's destroyed."

Sabrina winced and said reluctantly, "Well, I'd be happy to do that, Great-Grandma . . . if I had it."

A moment of chaos broke out. Great-Grandma threw up her arms and fell back against the back of the sofa.

Aunt Hilda shot to her feet and put a hand over her mouth as she gasped and said, "Oh, no!"

"You lost it, Sabrina?" Aunt Zelda called down from the corner.

"I'm sorry!" Sabrina cried. "You have no idea what kind of day I've had. It's been awful!"

"You have no idea where the pouch might be?" Aunt Zelda asked from above.

Aunt Hilda curled her fingers over her chin nervously and asked, "Do you think someone took it?"

Instead of answering them, Sabrina stared at

Great-Grandma's limp form on the sofa. "Do you think I should take her pulse?" she asked.

"I'm fine, dear, don't worry," Great-Grandma said quietly, without moving. She didn't even open her eyes. After a moment she sat up slowly and blinked her eyes a few times. "Hilda?"

"Yes, Great-Grandma?"

The old woman waved a hand, and Aunt Hilda floated up into the corner across from Aunt Zelda.

"What did I do?" Aunt Hilda cried into the corner, kicking her feet against the wall.

"I can't believe you two allowed this to happen," Great-Grandma said. "You should be ashamed. You're both staying up there until I say otherwise, and don't speak unless you're spoken to! You're being punished!" She looked up at Sabrina and patted the sofa cushion next to her. "Sit down, dear. Tell me the rest of your story."

Sabrina told her everything, including the weird things that had happened at school . . . the mysterious appearance of an elephant outside the cafeteria, and how Mr. Kraft got lost after a student wished that he would get lost . . . right up to the point where she lost the pouch.

Sabrina had searched hard for the wishdust, desperately covering every inch of the classroom. After finding nothing there, she'd searched the hall outside the classroom. By then, someone had managed to shut off the sprinkler system, and Sabrina headed straight for the administration office. Mrs. Mettwurst, the short, round secretary, stood behind the counter looking like a drowned muskrat. Sabrina described the pouch to her and asked Mrs. Mettwurst to please let her know if someone brought it in to the lost-and-found box.

"I'll do my best," Mrs. Mettwurst said in a quivering, mousey voice. "But it would be a lot easier if there were three of me . . . or half a dozen of me. Things have been so terribly busy around here, and now . . . well . . ." She looked around the office, ". . . things are so terribly wet."

Before Sabrina could leave, Mr. Kraft had stepped out of his office and called to her. She'd spun around, quickly told him all about the pouch, and asked him to please keep an eye open for it, then said, "Gotta go!" She'd hurried away before he could start questioning her about the sprinklers.

Sabrina told Great-Grandma how she'd searched the halls on her way out of the building . . . but the pouch had been nowhere in sight. It was simply gone!

When she was finished telling her story, Sabrina took in a deep breath and released a long sigh. She felt exhausted. It had been a long, unpleasant day.

Great-Grandma put an arm around Sabrina

and said, "Well, sweetie, I have good news and bad news. The good news is that I've known a few people who've been in the exact position you're in now. Not many, mind you, because the Witch Council made wishdust nearly impossible to find centuries ago. But it's been my experience that almost all of those people—not all, but almost all—have managed to find the wishdust before any serious damage was done. So, the statistics are in your favor. You've just got to try hard to find it."

"What's the bad news?" Sabrina asked.

"The bad news is that there's not a thing I can do to help you. You're on your own. That wishdust is yours . . . and you have to find it. No one else can help you out with this one. You can't use your magic against the powers of the wishdust . . . but you can use it to find the wishdust. Why don't you look up a finding spell in your spellbook?"

"Oh, no," Sabrina said, shaking her head. "The last time I did that, I nearly ended up married to a troll."

"Really? Was his name Roland, by any chance?"

"Yes. Have you heard of him?"

"Who hasn't? Somebody needs to teach that little masher a lesson."

"So, I've got to figure this one out myself, huh?"

"I'm afraid so. It's a little like being an adult, all of a sudden." She looked up, and her eyes bounced back and forth between the two occupied corners. "Something your aunts could take a lesson in, it seems." Looking at Sabrina again, she said, "But I think I can help you with something. Tell me about the woman who sold you the wishdust."

Sabrina described in great detail the old woman and her bizarre pet. Great-Grandma's eyes widened slowly with recognition.

"Salome Pettyjohn," Great-Grandma said.

"You know her?"

"Sweetheart, when you're as old as I am, you know just about everyone, whether you want to or not." She shook her head and clicked her tongue. "Salome Pettyjohn never had a moment of honesty or integrity in her entire life. And her entire life is almost as long as mine! If she ever tried to tell the truth, it would turn into a lie before it was out of her mouth. And if she ever tried to do a good deed . . . well, the sun would probably explode." She reached over and took Sabrina's hand. "When you find that wishdust, Sabrina . . . and I have great confidence that you will . . . I'll take it off your hands. I'll take it to the Witch Council. Along with Salome Pettyjohn. In a fishbowl. She won't get away with this, dear . . . I'll see to it." She looked up at Sabrina's aunts again and raised her voice slightly as she said, "Just as I'm seeing to it that certain other witches with problems in judgment and responsibility aren't getting away with that."

"Well . . . thanks, Great-Grandma. For the encouragement, at least."

"You're welcome, dear. You just focus your attention on that wishdust, use all the resources available to you, and don't stop until you've found it. Or until it destroys civilization as you know it. Whichever comes first." She grinned.

Sabrina felt herself shrink inside.

☆

Chapter 9

☆

The Monday Sabrina lost her pleather pouch of wishdust was the first day of a week that seemed to go on forever. It seemed to last even longer than an algebra test.

Sabrina got very little sleep on Monday night. All she could think about was the wishdust and who might have it . . . and those thoughts were so loud, they kept her awake most of the night. At some point during the wee hours of the morning, Salem wandered in and hopped onto her bed.

"You're tossing around so much in here," he said, "you're keeping me awake. And we cats sleep twenty hours a day!"

"You've got pretty good hearing, too," Sabrina said.

"Well, that goes without saying. Why don't

you try a sleeping spell? Or some of the sleeping powder from Zelda's Lab-Top?"

"No, I don't want to do that. I can't sleep because I'm worried about the wishdust, so if I'm awake, I might think of something."

"Think of something like what?"

"Well . . . who might have it. I mean, it just disappeared from that room, and I was the last one to leave."

"But who was still in the room when you fell and lost your purse?" Salem asked.

"I was too busy falling and losing my purse to notice."

"Then you need to ask everyone."

"Everyone? You mean, everyone in the class?"

"Why not everyone in the school? Couldn't you use the public address system?"

"Are you kidding? Mr. Kraft would rather shave his head than let me do something like that. But I can ask everyone in my algebra class if they saw the pouch or picked it up."

"There you go. That's what you should do."

She started first thing Tuesday morning, as soon as she got to school. Sabrina began asking the other students in her algebra class if they'd seen her pouch. All of them said no.

Valerie was present for most of the questioning, and she became curious.

"Okay, Sabrina, what's up?" she asked.

"What do you mean?"

"This pouch you keep talking about . . . what's in it?"

"In it? Um, well . . . nothing, really. It's just a . . . well, sorta like a change purse. But it's a-a-a . . . like a family heirloom."

Valerie frowned with suspicion. "Is that what you were so worried about?"

"Worried about? When?"

"Yesterday. You seemed really worried about something in your purse. Remember? When we were in the restroom?"

Sabrina's eyes widened slowly as she turned away from Valerie and stared at a wall of lockers across the corridor for a long moment. Yes, she remembered . . . and she also remembered thinking that Valerie was wearing glittery make-up. She put the two together and realized that some of the dust must have spilled from her purse as it was being passed to her down the line of girls standing in front of the mirror in the restroom. It must have spilled into all those open compacts on the counter, and that was where the elephant had come from . . . that was why Mr. Kraft had gotten lost at the wish of a student . . . and that was how Valerie had managed to wish the day to an end by inadvertently setting off the indoor sprinkler system.

"Hey, uh . . . Sabrina? You okay?" Valerie asked.

"I'm fine," Sabrina said, turning back to her friend suddenly. "Let me see your compact."

"What? My—"

"Your compact, come on, let me see it!" Sabrina's voice was full of urgency, and her face glowed with excitement.

Valerie reached into her purse and handed the compact over, looking at Sabrina as if she were wearing a monkey suit.

"When was the last time you used this?" Sabrina asked as she opened Valerie's compact.

"Uh . . . this morning, I guess."

Sure enough, there were still sparkling traces of the wishdust visible inside the compact. There wasn't much . . . just a few tiny grains of the wishdust left. Sabrina wondered if it was enough to use . . . enough to wish the pouch back into her possession.

Sabrina looked at Valerie, about to ask if she could borrow her compact for a while, but Valerie's face had changed. She had become zombiefied. Her eyes were wide, and her mouth had fallen open as she looked at something behind Sabrina.

Someone tapped on Sabrina's shoulder, and she turned around.

There were four people standing in front of her, two young women and two young men. The younger of the two couples wore regular, every-day clothes. But the other couple looked different . . . and they didn't look like much of a couple. The young woman wore a tennis outfit, carried a tennis racket, and had a thin sheen of perspiration on her face. The young man was shirtless and barefoot, with mussed blond hair, and wore white pajama bottoms with thin blue stripes.

Sabrina recognized them and gasped, dropping the compact to the floor. It hit with a loud clatter.

"Excuse me," Leonardo DiCaprio said with a pleasant smile. "Could you tell us where we might find a phone?"

Neve Campbell scratched her head and said, "We were shooting a movie in a town near here, and . . . well, I don't know what happened, but all of a sudden we were . . . here!"

"I was playing tennis in Santa Barbara," Winona Ryder said, looking confused.

Brad Pitt yawned, and said, "And I was asleep in my hotel room . . . in Germany. I'm shooting a movie there. But now . . ." He shrugged and yawned again.

Sabrina and Valerie were sort of yawning, too . . . but not from sleepiness. They had lost control of their jaws, and their mouths were hanging open. Slowly . . . very slowly . . . both of the girls raised their arms and pointed in the direction of the main office.

"Thank you," Leonardo DiCaprio said with a nod and another pleasant smile.

The four movie stars turned and headed in the direction indicated.

After all those rumors about a movie being made near here, Sabrina thought, *somebody accidentally wished them here!*

Valerie began to walk slowly in the direction the celebrities had gone.

"Where are you going?" Sabrina asked.

"I'm going to make sure they find the office," Valerie said. She stopped and turned to Sabrina. "And then I'm going to marry either Leonardo DiCaprio or Brad Pitt and live happily ever after." She hurried after the movie stars.

Sabrina looked down at the compact on the floor. It had shattered over the tiles, and so had the pale cake of face powder inside. The powder had broken in many tiny pieces, some of which had disintegrated into crumb-size bits and some even smaller. She fished through the remains, but couldn't find the tiny grains of wishdust.

The rest of the day at school was chaotic. Word spread like wildfire that the celebrities were there, and everybody went nuts. But no one besides Sabrina and Valerie actually saw the movie stars. They had somehow disappeared. Sabrina was sure they'd been sneaked out of the school safely, and she suspected nothing more would be heard about the incident.

When she wasn't in classes, Sabrina continued to ask people from her algebra class if they'd seen her pouch, but she got nothing but no's from them. She also made a list of the girls she remembered being in the restroom the day before, when her purse had been passed down the line and some of the wishdust had spilled into the makeup compacts on the counter. It was a short list, and she wasn't sure if she'd remembered all the girls in the restroom . . . but it would have to do. Walking alone on her way to the cafeteria at lunchtime, Sabrina wadded the list in her hand and whispered a spell.

"Compacts of powder, eye shadow, and rouge,
rush into my purse with the speed of a luge."

Sabrina's purse suddenly became a bit heavier. The spell she'd just cast had sent the compacts from the purse of each girl on the list to Sabrina's purse. She ducked into a restroom, found a stall, closed and locked the door, then carefully inspected each of the compacts in her purse.

There wasn't a speck of wishdust in any of them.

"This is not cool," Sabrina muttered, waving a

hand and sending all the compacts back to their owners.

> "Back to the purses where you all were,
> stealthy and silent, without even a stir."

If she'd found some wishdust, she could have used it to wish the pouch back into her possession. But now, she was going to have to continue asking around, hoping someone could point her in the right direction and, for the most part, relying on luck.

Harvey hadn't seen the pouch. Neither had Mark, whom Sabrina had nearly forgotten about in the panic of searching for her wishdust. He told her he still wanted to talk and asked when she would have some free time. She answered him honestly and said she didn't know, but assured him she wanted to talk, too, and would get together with him as soon as possible. She hoped he was planning to ask her to the dance. If she had the wishdust, she'd use it to make certain that's what he wanted to ask her . . . but by the end of the day, she still didn't have it.

Sabrina arrived at school early the next morning to continue searching. She didn't get very far into the main building, though.

"Miss Spellman," Mr. Kraft called from the

doorway of the main office. "Could you come into my office please?"

Sabrina's blood froze in her veins as she turned to the vice-principal. She smiled and asked, "You found it, then?"

Mr. Kraft smiled back, but without humor. "Very funny. Please come with me, Miss Spellman."

In the office, Sabrina sat in the chair facing the vice-principal's desk, but Mr. Kraft remained standing. He paced slowly behind the desk, keeping his eyes on her.

"We had some very interesting visitors here yesterday, Miss Spellman," he said. "Maybe you heard about it. Four movie stars?"

"Movie stars?" Sabrina asked, feigning innocence and ignorance.

"That's right. Surely you know who I'm talking about."

"Uh . . . Robert De Niro? Faye Dunaway? Jack Nicholson?"

Mr. Kraft frowned as he continued to pace. "Don't toy with me, Miss Spellman. You know as well as I do who they were. Two of them were shooting a movie outside of town. The other two were, uh . . . shall we say . . . way outside of town. In fact, one of them was out of the country. Quite suddenly, they found themselves here, at Westbridge High. No cars were involved . . . no buses, no planes . . . just boom, they were here. We got them off campus immediately and agreed not to talk to the press about their mysterious appearance here . . . but I'm talking to you about it because I strongly suspect you know something about it."

"Why would you think that, Mr. Kraft?"

"Because you always seem to be close whenever something weird happens. Weird things have been happening lately, Miss Spellman, and I would like you to explain them."

"I wish I could, but . . . I can't." She tried not to wince. After all, it was a lie . . . but she couldn't tell him the truth!

Mr. Kraft stopped pacing and turned to face her with his hands locked behind his back. "I don't believe you. But there's nothing I can do about it right now."

"Well, uh, Mr. Kraft . . . I've gotta go." She started to stand.

"Wait just a second."

Sabrina lowered herself back into the chair, frustrated that she'd failed at making a clean getaway.

Mr. Kraft asked, "Did you ever find that little purse you were looking for, Miss Spellman?"

Sabrina shot to her feet, and her face brightened as she asked, "Did you find it?"

"No, I didn't. I'm asking if you did."

Her shoulders slumped, and the brightness

drained from her face. "No. I haven't found it yet."

"Well, let's say I did find it, Miss Spellman. If I did . . . would you be willing to tell me the truth in exchange for it?"

"The truth about what?" Sabrina asked warily.

"The truth about you, Miss Spellman." He began pacing again, but continued to watch her. "You see, I know there's something funny about you. Something odd, something not right. I just haven't figured out what it is yet. So, let's say I find that purse for you, that family heirloom. If I do that"—he suddenly stopped pacing, planted his flat palms on his desktop, and leaned toward her—"will you finally tell me whatever it is you're not telling me now? Will you finally tell me what in the world is wrong with you?"

"I don't know what you're talking about, Mr. Kraft." She stood. "And I really have to go. But if you do find that purse, I hope you'll be decent enough to let me know and hand it over."

He stood up straight and smiled cunningly at her. "We'll see, Miss Spellman. We'll see."

Sabrina left the office and hurried down the hall. She was shaken by the possibility that Mr. Kraft might find the pouch first and withhold it from her until she told him . . . well, something. Maybe she could tell him she was an alien from outer space trying to fit in with American teenagers. He'd probably believe it and would, no doubt, end up making a fool of himself. But she would rather find the pouch first and avoid any complications with that nimrod of a vice-principal.

As Sabrina hurried down the hall, Mr. Kraft picked up the receiver of his telephone and punched the two buttons that would connect him with Mr. Edgerly, the janitor. When the phone at the other end was answered, Mr. Kraft said, "Hello, Edgerly. This is Mr. Kraft. I'd like you to look very carefully around the school for something I've lost. It's a purse. . . ."

By lunchtime Sabrina had gotten nowhere in finding the wishdust. To make the day even worse, she learned that Mark was home sick. She hoped he'd be well enough to go to the dance . . . especially if he was going to ask her to go with him!

Sabrina stopped just inside the cafeteria and looked around for her friends. She spotted Harvey and Valerie talking animatedly over their lunches near the windows. Sabrina noticed the cafeteria was louder than usual and scanned the other students sitting at the tables. They, too, were excited about something, and many of them kept gesturing to the lunch trays before them. Sabrina got in line and took a tray from the stack.

A lot of noise came from the kitchen . . . more

than the usual clattering and chattering. People were shouting back there.

"Who's the comedian?" Mr. Gurber shouted angrily.

Mrs. Poupiepenz replied, "It wasn't me! You think I'd make this stuff? Hah!"

Sabrina recognized the large woman's voice immediately. It was so loud, it was hard not to recognize. Sabrina had dealt with her before . . . and had a tendency to accidentally call her Mrs. Poopy Pants.

"I wouldn't make this stuff!" Mrs. Poupiepenz continued. "Especially not on Salisbury steak day, and today is Salisbury steak day! Hot fudge sundaes . . . hah!"

Hot fudge sundaes? Sabrina thought. She didn't know what was going on, but she had a bad feeling about it.

The others in line ahead of her were laughing and saying things like, "All right!" and, "This is so cool!" and, "Whoever had this idea should get a raise!"

Sabrina stepped up in line, and two things were placed on her tray: a steaming pile of scrumptuous-looking barbecued ribs, and a beautiful hot fudge sundae covered with whipped cream and nuts, and topped with two fat, glistening cherries.

"Ooohhh, boy," Sabrina muttered to herself. "Somebody made a really weird wish."

That had to be it . . . a frivolous wish made by someone who, at that very moment, unknowingly had some wishdust on his or her fingertips. At least, Sabrina hoped it was done unknowingly. If someone had already figured out what the wishdust was and how it worked—very unlikely, but with the luck Sabrina had been having, not entirely out of the question—then she was in even bigger trouble.

Luck, she thought grimly, *I remember when my lucky rabbit's foot was passed around school. Why do my magic talismen get passed around faster than a cold?*

She took her tray to the table where Harvey and Valerie were enjoying their unusual lunch.

"Can you believe this, Sabrina?" Valerie asked, grinning.

"I used to think my grandpa made the best barbecued ribs in the world," Harvey said. Barbecue sauce glistened at the corners of his mouth. "But these blow his away! Mrs. Poupiepenz did an incredible job!"

Valerie took a bite of her sundae. A moment later, she rolled her eyes and licked her lips. "This is theeee best hot fudge sundae I've ever had! If Ben and Jerry made it themselves, it couldn't be this good! I wonder what kind of ice cream Mrs. Poupiepenz used."

Sabrina stared at the delicious-looking food before her . . . but she didn't feel very hungry all of a sudden. "I don't think it was intentional," she said quietly.

Harvey frowned at her. "It wasn't intentional? Well, uh . . . then how do you accidentally serve barbecued ribs and hot fudge sundaes to a whole school for lunch?"

"And on Salisbury steak day, no less," Valerie added.

Sabrina decided it was time to change the subject quickly. "How's everything coming for the dance, Valerie?"

"Really well. But we're not going to be able to afford everything we need. Mr. Kraft nearly exploded when we told him how much more glitter we wanted."

"Glitter?" Sabrina asked.

Harvey listened, but was too busy chewing on barbecued ribs to participate in the conversation.

"For the decorations," Valerie replied. "Libby's theme is 'The Warm Weather Snow Ball.' See, we wanted to make the whole gym look like the poster for the dance, the one hanging in the hall just outside the administration office. You know how the word *snow* turns into those long icicles along the bottom? And how we put glitter on the icicles to make them look like real ice, all sparkly and wet? Well, we wanted to do that with the whole gym. I mean, don't you think that would be so cool? But we don't have enough stuff, and Mr. Kraft nearly popped an artery when we asked so . . ." She shrugged, then took another chocolatey bite of her hot fudge sundae.

"Are you okay, Sabrina?" Harvey asked. "You look . . . I don't know . . . upset or depressed, or something."

She smiled and said, "Just . . . preoccupied, I guess."

"Did you ever find that bag you were looking for?" he asked.

Sabrina shook her head no, then tried again to change the subject quickly. "Who are you taking to the dance, Harvey?"

"Charlotte Wanamaker. How about you? Who're you going with?"

"Nobody's asked yet. What about you, Valerie?"

"I'm going with Lawrence Roddencone," she said, with no enthusiasm whatsoever.

"Really?" Sabrina said. "I've never even seen you two talking."

"We haven't. But nobody else asked me, so I figured . . . why not?" Valerie frowned slightly. "But it would be more fun, I think, if I could get him to take that ugly white tape off his broken glasses and talk about something besides *Babylon 5*."

The ribs and sundae were both delicious, but Sabrina had lost her appetite and could manage no more than a couple bites of each. She continued to ask around about the pouch for the rest of the day, but no one had so much as glimpsed it. She was glad to see the day end.

On her way out of the building, Sabrina stopped to look at the poster for the Snow Ball. It was very pretty. But if she was unable to find the wishdust, she didn't know if she was going to feel up to going to a dance, whether Mark asked her or not.

Maybe she'd just stay home and watch television. There were some funny shows on Friday night . . . and Sabrina could use a good laugh.

The first thing Sabrina saw when she got to school on Thursday morning was a very confused looking Santa Claus standing at the top of the front steps out of the rain. He kept looking around, scratching his head, looking around . . . as if he were lost.

Uh-oh, Sabrina thought as she passed him. *Looks like somebody's been wishing it were Christmas-time.*

"Sabrina!" Santa called. "How nice to see you again!"

"Hello, Santa. What are you, um . . . doing here?"

"Well, I . . . I . . ." He stroked his beard and frowned for a moment, then gave her a smile. "I have no idea. But I'm sure Mrs. Claus won't be happy about it. Her toaster oven's on the blink, and I was supposed to fix it today."

"Can I help you? I mean, is there anything I can do?"

"Oh, no," he said firmly. "You have classes, Sabrina. That's important. You've always been a good student, and I wouldn't want to stand in the way of that." He gave her a charming wink. "I'll, uh . . . I'll figure this out and get myself home somehow. You take care."

She gave him a smile as she went inside, then went to her locker. Suddenly, above the chatter that was going on all around her in the hall, Sabrina heard an unmistakable, steel-edged voice.

"How could you make such a stupid mistake?" the voice barked at someone. "I don't know if we'll ever be able to get a decent band on such short notice!"

"I'm sorry, Libby," Valerie said. "It was a mistake, I know, but I'll do my best to fix it and—"

Sabrina turned around and saw Libby Chessler stalking down the hall looking furious. Valerie, who looked miserable, was trying hard to keep up with her. Libby stopped and turned on Valerie, saying, "You will not do anything! You've done enough, thank you very much. Just leave it to those of us who know what we're doing." Then she went down the hall like an angry army drill instructor.

"What happened?" Sabrina asked as Valerie approached her despondently.

"I've ruined my reputation," Valerie said.

"I didn't know you *had* a reputation." Poor Valerie. Despite her aspirations, Sabrina suspected Val would never make a dent in Libby's social circles.

"Well, I do now, and it's a bad one. I made a mistake. A big mistake. The kind of mistake that would probably get me executed in some countries."

And then there's her tendency to exaggerate . . .

As they walked together, Sabrina asked Valerie to tell her all about it.

"One of my responsibilities on the committee was to get the band," Valerie said. "Since the theme of the dance is snow, I thought it would be cool to get a band that would tie in with that. You know . . . maybe a band that had a wintery-sounding name. Well, I finally came up with one. They call themselves Frozen Tundra. Sounded great to me. I talked to the band's manager, which wasn't easy because he spoke with a really thick accent I didn't recognize and he didn't speak very good English. But the band charged below the music budget, so I made all the arrangements."

"And what did Libby find wrong with all of that?"

"Well . . . she found out that the band doesn't exactly play the kind of music we were looking for. They play, um . . . oh, this is so embarassing."

"What? What do they play?"

"Latvian folk songs."

"Latvian? But . . . why do they call themselves Frozen Tundra?"

"Well, it sounded like Frozen Tundra to me . . . but the band manager's accent was so thick and his English was so bad . . ."

"Don't tell me. The band's manager speaks Latvian."

"Apparently. What sounded like 'Frozen Tundra' to me was really something in Latvian that referred to a particular folk song and . . . and the animal they have in their act."

"Animal? What kind of animal?"

"A yak."

"Ah. Not good Snow Ball material."

"Now Libby and all the others hate me. They hated it when Ms. O'Connor pushed me onto the dance committee . . . and now I've proven they were right, and they hate me even more."

"Look, Valerie," Sabrina said, "being hated by Libby and her fashion cult isn't such a bad thing. It shows you've got good character." She put an arm around her friend's shoulders consolingly.

"And don't worry about making a mistake. We all do it." She sighed heavily. "I sure have made my share of 'em."

Mark came up behind them and appeared at Sabrina's side. "Hi, you two. How's it going?"

"I'm doomed," Valerie said.

Sabrina gave her a friendly poke with an elbow and said, "Oh, stop it. The dance will be great, and you and Lawrence Roddencone will have a lot of fun."

"Oh, that's right!" Valerie gasped. "I've gotta go find him. I'm gonna try to talk him into letting me glue his broken glasses before the dance. He's a really nice guy, don't get me wrong, but . . . he looks like such a dork what with that big lump of white tape between his eyes. See you guys later!" Valerie hurried off, her doomed reputation apparently forgotten for the moment.

"I'm glad you're feeling better," Sabrina said, turning to Mark.

"When I woke up yesterday morning, I felt like I'd gone a few rounds with Mike Tyson."

"How are your ears?"

He laughed. "It was just a twenty-four hour bug, though. And I'm glad, because we still haven't had a chance to talk."

"We could meet for lunch," Sabrina suggested.

"I'd rather talk now, if you don't mind. I'd like to . . . well, if you haven't . . ."

Sabrina stopped walking and turned to him.

She tilted her head to one side and smiled. Not only was Mark very nervous, not quite meeting her eyes as he shifted his weight from one foot to the other and back, he was *blushing*.

How cute.

Mark cleared his throat and continued, "What I mean is, if you don't already . . . you know, have a date . . . I'd really like to take you to the dance tomorrow night."

Sabrina's smile became a grin as she took Mark's hand and said, "I'd love to go with you!"

He got a sort of aw-shucks look to him for a moment, then they started walking together. But he held on to her hand.

"I should warn you, though," he said, "I'm not a very good dancer. My sister says that, on the dance floor, I look like a wounded ostrich."

"Hey, that's cool!" Sabrina said with laughter in her eyes. "The ostrich is my favorite bird!"

Although she continued to search for the pouch of wishdust that day, Sabrina's luck was no better than it had been the rest of the week. But on that day, she actually felt good for a change, and she couldn't stop thinking about how much fun it would be to go to the Warm Weather Snow Ball with Mark.

Chapter 10

☆

By the end of school on Thursday, Mr. Kraft was in a very cranky mood. It had been a weird week and a busy day. He was behind in his work because, for one thing, he'd had to call the police and have them escort some confused wacko in a Santa Claus suit off the school grounds, and for another . . . although days had passed since he'd first become mysteriously lost in the school's main building, he still tended to get lost on the way to his office. Late that morning, he'd ended up in a janitorial closet. It was very aggravating. He had to stay late to finish his work, so he made Mrs. Mettwurst stay late to file his work.

"All right, I'll stay," Mrs. Mettwurst said. "But I'm telling you, Mr. Kraft, it's been getting awfully busy around here lately. It would help if

I were a few more people, if you know what I mean."

Mr. Kraft smiled. "Of course, Mrs. Mettwurst. And as soon as I can find a few more of you, I'll see that they're hired . . . if you know what I mean." He went back into his office and sat behind his desk and got to work.

Two hours later, after all the students and nearly all the faculty and staff had left the school, there was a knock at Mr. Kraft's office door.

"Come in, Mrs. Mettwurst," Mr. Kraft called.

The door opened, but it was Mr. Edgerly who leaned into the office.

"Mr. Kraft? You said to look around for a leather pouch, right? Well, I found this." He stepped into the office and held up a pouch of mottled leather, drawn together at the top by a thick string.

Mr. Kraft's eyes slowly widened and his mouth peeled back over his teeth, first in a smile, then a grin, then in something so wide that it threatened dangerously to lop off the top half of his head.

"Why, thank you, Mr. Edgerly!" Mr. Kraft exclaimed as he stood, hurried around the desk and plucked the pouch from Mr. Edgerly's grasp, then shook the janitor's hand. "Where did you find it?"

"In the shrubs just outside the rear doors of the main building."

"Wonderful. Wonderful!" Mr. Kraft patted Mr. Edgerly on the back. "This is so great, Edgerly, I just might look into getting a raise for you!"

Mr. Edgerly's weathered face burst into a grin. "You think so, Mr. Kraft?"

Still smiling, the vice-principal said, "Probably not. See you later."

By the time Mr. Kraft was seated behind his desk again, Mr. Edgerly had left and closed the door behind him. Mr. Kraft put the pouch on his desk and stared at it.

"That's some weird, tacky-looking leather," he said to himself. "Looks like it came from a sick cow. Last cow I saw that had mottled coloring like this was a poorly cooked hamburger."

He wondered what was in it. Miss Spellman had been looking for it with great desperation lately, as if it were very important to her. Maybe it was something important . . . something he could use to get the truth out of her . . . the truth about her!

Mr. Kraft leaned forward and lifted the little bag, then pulled the top open with thumb and forefinger. He peered in . . . and made a grunting sound.

"Glitter?" he asked himself.

He reached into the pouch with the thumb and first finger of his right hand and scooped out some of the contents. It was quite beautiful . . . a pinch of sparkling iridescence.

"But it's just glitter!" he snapped at no one in particular as he tossed the tiny pieces of multi-colored light into the air angrily.

For such a small pinch, it went everywhere . . . on the desk, on the floor, on him. He grumbled as he wheeled backward in his chair, telling himself, "Well, that was smart."

He'd been hoping for something he could use against Miss Spellman, something that might be important enough to her for her to spill the truth to him. Obviously, he'd been grasping at straws.

He stood suddenly and decided he'd worked long enough for one day. He was hungry and decided to stop on the way home for a good old-fashioned restaurant-cooked meal. He picked up the pouch from his desk, pulled the drawstring and closed it, then left his office.

"Mrs. Mettwurst," he called.

She hurried toward him from the filing cabinet. "Yes, Mr. Kraft? Are we going home now?"

"Well, I am. I expect you to finish the filing before you leave. Here, take this." He handed her the pouch. "Give this to the dance committee. They were griping about not having enough glitter the other day, maybe this'll make them happy. Have a good evening, Mrs. Mettwurst." And then he was gone.

"Have a good evening filing, you mean," Mrs.

Mettwurst muttered, looking at the pouch. Curious, she carefully opened the pouch and looked inside.

"I'm a failure, Salem," Sabrina said as she flopped onto her bed. "A complete and utter failure."

Salem hopped onto the bed and settled down right in front of her face, looking her straight in the eyes.

"Listen to me, Sabrina. I come from a long line of failures. Did you know that my father invented what he called the ultimate witch's tool? It was a broom for flying, a ladle for stirring and scooping stuff from the cauldron, and a hatrack for hanging your hat after you got home from flying around."

"Sounds like a good idea."

"Yeah, but the broom was at one end, the ladle was at the other, and the hat hooks were in between. The stupid thing wouldn't stand up. He went broke."

"What does that mean?"

"It means a hatrack should be able to stand up, otherwise it's kind of useless. My great-grandfather invented a passion potion."

"Passion potion?"

"Passion potion. It was like a love potion, only ten times more powerful. It was supposed to make the person of your dreams fall passionately in love with you."

"What happened?"

"It worked. But unfortunately, it also made the subject terribly nauseated. So, the person who was supposed to fall passionately in love with you did . . . but he'd barf his head off at the sight of you."

"Not good."

"Well, there was a small sect of people in the ninth dimension who found nausea romantic . . . but beyond that, no, not good. It was a horrible disaster."

"Why are you telling me this, Salem?"

"Because you shouldn't worry about failing, Sabrina. Like my father and my great-grandfather, you tried your best, and that really means something. It doesn't mean you're a bad person just because you can't find a pouch full of wishdust."

"It may not mean I'm a bad person," Sabrina said. "But it could mean the end of the world as we know it! I mean, who knows what people are wishing for out there while they've got a little wishdust on their fingers?"

"Yeah, who knows? Maybe somebody will wish for a cure for cancer or an end to world hunger! Have you thought of that?"

"At Westbridge High? Are you kidding? So far,

we've gotten an elephant, indoor rain, four movie stars, barbecued ribs, hot fudge sundaes, and Santa Claus."

Salem sighed. "Apparently, youth is wasted on the stupid." He stood and arched his back, then stretched his back legs. "Well, don't worry too much. It's not good for you." He headed for the foot of the bed.

"Where are you going?"

Salem stopped and turned to her. "To get some Lizard Flakes. That's one really good thing you did, Sabrina." He walked back to her and licked her nose. "You made me a very happy cat." Then he hopped off the bed and left the room.

Mr. Kraft returned home from his dinner to the yapping of his ex-wife's Chihuahua, Tico. The dog was just about the only thing she'd let him keep. Tico yapped at his heels as he went into the living room, flopped into his recliner, picked up the remote control, and turned on the television. He was still wearing his suit, but he was too exhausted to change clothes. He just wanted to let *Wheel of Fortune* numb his brain a bit before he slipped into his around-the-house sweats.

Tico continued to yap and yap and yap.

"Yeah, yeah," Mr. Kraft said. "I'll feed you in just a second. I promise."

The Chihuahua stopped yapping, settled down on his haunches, and stared up at Mr. Kraft with big, glistening eyes.

After a few minutes, Mr. Kraft's head began to nod, until it fell forward and his chin rested on his chest. He woke himself up from his doze with his own snore, which startled his eyes open wide and made his whole body jerk. Tico was, in turn, startled by this sudden movement and ran away with a yelp.

Mr. Kraft left the recliner and went to his bedroom, where he changed out of his suit and into his robe and slippers. As he hung up the suit, he spotted glitter on the front of the suitcoat. It was the glitter from Miss Spellman's odd little bag . . . Miss Spellman, whom he was *certain* was different from all the other students at Westbridge High. There was something not quite right about her, and as he brushed the glitter from his suitcoat, he wished he could get Sabrina Spellman to tell him the truth about herself so he wouldn't have to wonder anymore.

He was heading into the kitchen to feed Tico when the telephone rang. Mr. Kraft picked up the cordless receiver, but the person on the other end didn't even give him a chance to say, "Hello."

"Is this Mr. Kraft?"

"Yes, who's this?"

"Sabrina Spellman. I'm calling to tell you the truth about myself."

Mr. Kraft frowned, blinked a few times, and asked, "And what's that, Miss Spellman?"

"I'm a witch."

"A witch. Well, isn't that . . . quaint."

"That's why I've ended up connected to so many weird things at school. They were all related to magic in one way or another."

"Magic. A witch." He lowered himself back into his recliner. "And how does one become a witch, Miss Spellman, tell me that?"

"Oh, it's a hereditary thing. My aunts told me on my sixteenth birthday."

"Your aunts?" The thought of Hilda Spellman made him go all gooey for a minute. "Are they witches, too?"

"Sure. And our cat is actually a warlock who tried to use his witchcraft to take over the world. But he got caught and was punished by being turned into a cat for a hundred years."

Mr. Kraft listened carefully to the voice on the other end of the line, just to make sure it really was Sabrina Spellman . . . and not someone pulling some insipid prank.

Tico appeared at Mr. Kraft's feet again and began yapping mercilessly.

"Yap-yap-YAP! Yap-yap-YAP! YAP-YAP-YAP-YAP!"

"Hush, Tico, hush!" Mr. Kraft barked. "All

right, Miss Spellman . . . prove to me you're a witch, if you don't mind."

"Prove it? Well . . . I can make your dog stop barking."

Mr. Kraft tilted his head back and laughed as Tico continued to yap sharply. "Oh, that's funny. I'm afraid nobody can make this dog stop—"

Tico fell silent.

Mr. Kraft leaned forward in his chair and looked down at the dog. Tico had curled up on the floor and looked quite content.

"See?" Miss Spellman said. "I just cast a little spell, and it worked. Your dog is quiet."

A chill passed down Mr. Kraft's spine. It wasn't a chill of fear, but one of excitement. A witch . . . a real witch!

"What inspired you to call me at home and tell me all this, Miss Spellman?" he asked.

"Well, I'm not sure. It's definitely not something I'd normally do. And there's a part of me, deep inside, that's panicking right now—I mean panicking big time—but it's a very tiny part. So, my best guess is that you found my pouch of wishdust and used it."

"Wish . . . dust?"

"Yes. Remember the pouch I was looking for? You found it, didn't you?"

"Well, uh . . . yes, I did."

"You looked inside and thought it was just glitter, didn't you?"

"Um, glitter. Yes. But what is it . . . really?"

"Wishdust. You sprinkle some in the air, make a wish, and . . . tah-dah! Your wish comes true."

Mr. Kraft closed his eyes and thought about what he had done only minutes ago. He had brushed the glitter from his suitcoat while wishing Sabrina would tell him the truth about herself . . . which was what she was doing right then!

"You're not pulling my leg, are you, Miss Spellman?" he asked quietly. "I mean, you wouldn't do that, would you?"

"I really don't have the least bit of interest in your leg, Mr. Kraft."

Mr. Kraft closed his eyes and mumbled to himself, "A witch . . . wishdust . . ."

"Well, I really have to go, Mr. Kraft. I've got some things to do."

"Wait, Miss Spellman, please. I'd just like to ask you—"

She hung up.

After a moment Mr. Kraft replaced the receiver. Wishdust . . . stuff that could make his wishes come true. And he'd had it! He'd had a pouch of wishdust right in his hands, but then . . . then . . . then what had he done with it? He thought a moment. That's right! He had told Mrs. Mettwurst to give it to the dance committee. He stood slowly—Tico still curled up at his feet—thrust his fists into the air, locked his elbows, and screamed, "What a stupid thing to dooooooo!"

Tico stood in an instant and began yapping again as Mr. Kraft grabbed his coat. He'd decided to go back to the school to see if he could retrieve the pouch.

Still lying on her bed, Sabrina hung up the phone. Almost immediately, whatever it was that had overtaken her passed, and she felt sick with dread.

"I can't believe I just did that," she whispered, sitting up straight. She got off the bed and said, again, "I can't . . . believe . . . I just did that! I just told Mr. Kraft everything he's always wanted to know . . . about me! What will he do? Who will he tell?"

Aunt Hilda leaned through the open door into Sabrina's bedroom. "Is something wrong, sweetie?"

"Everything is wrong, Aunt Hilda." Sabrina put a hand to her chest and began taking deep, slow breaths. "I've ruined everything! I've ruined us all!"

"Calm down, calm down. Sabrina, dear, what are you talking about?" Aunt Hilda put an arm around Sabrina's shoulder and pulled her down until they were sitting on the edge of the bed together.

Salem sauntered into the room, hopped onto the bed with them, and began cleaning his whiskers.

"I just called Mr. Kraft at home and told him I'm a witch," Sabrina said, her voice filled with defeat.

"You did what?" Aunt Hilda blurted.

"Wait, wait just a second," Salem said. "Let me get this straight. You were just sitting around here in your bedroom, and you decided, all of a sudden, to call up your vice-principal and say . . . what? 'Hi, Mr. Kraft, it's Sabrina. Guess what? I'm a witch! See you tomorrow in home-room!'"

Sabrina gave a heavy sigh and closed her eyes. "No . . . not just that. I told him my aunts are witches, too," Sabrina went on. "I even told him all about you, Salem. And the whole time I was doing it I didn't want to do it. But I had no choice. I was being forced."

"Oh, no, Sabrina!" Aunt Hilda exclaimed. "Why would you tell him such a thing?"

"What could force you to tell him all those things, Sabrina?" Salem asked.

"Wishdust. He found my pouch of wishdust, and somehow . . . he wished it. He's always been suspicious of me, he's always thought there was something different about me, something funny. And even though he didn't know what was in that pouch, he somehow managed to use it to wish that I would tell him the truth about myself."

"Oh, dear," Aunt Hilda whispered, touching four fingers to her lower lip. "You know what this means, don't you, Sabrina? Now that he knows the truth about you . . . about all of us . . . you can't reverse it with a spell. You can't make him lose his memory, or anything else like that . . . because your magic is powerless against the work of the wishdust. So's mine. So's everyone's! Oh, no . . . this sort of thing can ruin a witch for . . . well, for life!"

Uh-oh. Sabrina's aunts were well over five hundred years old. "For life" had a *whole* different meaning when one was a witch.

"Unless I get that wishdust back," Sabrina said. "I think I can . . . if he's still got it. If he doesn't have it anymore . . . well, then, I'll just have to keep looking, the way I've been looking all week. It's out there somewhere!"

As Mr. Kraft parked his car in front of the main building, he was surprised to see the administration office all lit up inside and the shadowy movements of a few people on the other side of the blinds. He left his car and ran through the rain and up the front steps of the school. Keys jangled as he found the right one, unlocked the glass doors, and ran into the building.

Five women, all dressed exactly alike, were

engaging in friendly chatter as they worked busily.

Mr. Kraft looked at them, watched them go back and forth from the file cabinet, the copy machine, the cupboards, and drawers. As he watched, he realized who the five women were.

"Mrs. Mettwurst?" he said with a crack in his voice.

All five women froze, turned to him, smiled, and said cheerfully, "Hello, Mr. Kraft!"

"Oh, no," Mr. Kraft groaned. For the last two or three weeks, Mrs. Mettwurst had been complaining about how busy things had been and complaining that she had no one to help her in the office. More than a few times he'd heard her remark that her job would be a lot easier if she could be more than one person . . . or if there were a half-dozen of her. Now there were . . . and Mr. Kraft was pretty sure he knew how she'd made it happen.

He counted the women quickly, realized there were five, not six, and wondered which one was the real Mrs. Mettwurst . . . if she was there at all.

"Mrs. Mettwurst?" he said again, more confidently this time.

"Yes?" all five women said simultaneously.

"Uh . . . that pouch I gave you this afternoon . . . what did you do with it?" he asked.

All the Mrs. Mettwursts looked at one another curiously for a moment, then one of them smiled and stepped forward.

"You must be looking for the original Mrs. Mettwurst," she said.

"Yes, as a matter of fact, I am," Mr. Kraft said, beginning to sound impatient.

"Oh, she went home a few hours ago. We stayed here to do what she made us to do. We'll probably be here all night."

"And what is that?"

"To work, of course. She's just got too much for one person to handle, so she copied herself and left us here to work all night and catch up."

"Well, working all night long is against regulations," Mr. Kraft made up on the spot. He lifted a finger and pointed it at the Mrs. Mettwurst who had been speaking to him. "And I'm not positive, but I'm willing to bet there's something in there against copying yourself, too! I'm going to find out, and when I do, I'm going to use it to kick all of you out of here! Because you . . . well, you, uh . . . frankly, you all . . . give me the creeps!" He spun around and hurried out of the office.

As he drove out of the school parking lot, he tried to remember where Mrs. Mettwurst lived. He'd dropped by her place once about a year ago . . . a small, cozy-looking house with a picket fence around the well-kept yard. It was just down the street from Snax and Gas convenience store.

Once he found the store, it was no problem locating Mrs. Mettwurst's house. There was no car in the driveway, and the house appeared dark . . . but maybe Mrs. Mettwurst and her husband weren't gone, maybe they'd just gone to bed early. Mr. Kraft had no problem with waking them up. He wanted that pouch.

Wishing he'd thought to bring an umbrella, he went through the front gate, up the walk and knocked on the door, getting wetter with each step. After several seconds, he knocked again. He heard no voices or movement in the house.

Mr. Kraft pounded hard on the door and shouted, "Mrs. Mettwurst? Mrs. Mettwurst! It's Mr. Kraft!"

When he got no response to that, he left the porch and went to one of the front windows. He knocked his knuckles on the windowpane and shouted for her again, but still heard nothing. They weren't home.

Grumbling under his breath, Mr. Kraft went around the corner of the house and found a tall wooden gate leading to the backyard. He stood there a moment, contemplating his options, and getting soaked in the rain.

He could sit in his car and wait for Mrs. Mettwurst and her husband to get back and then ask her about the pouch. Or, he could make his way into the house somehow and try to find it himself. Either way, he had to get that pouch back—providing Mrs. Mettwurst still had it—because it was just too dangerous in the hands of someone who didn't know what it was. He realized that was the reason for all the weirdness at school lately . . . elephants and movie stars, sprinklers going off, a student wishing Mr. Kraft would get lost just seconds before he actually did get lost. All those things had happened because Sabrina had lost her pouch of wishdust, and it had been bouncing all over school! Mr. Kraft couldn't let that continue.

He opened the gate and walked through, then turned and closed it again.

It was very dark, so Mr. Kraft felt his way along the side of the house. When he rounded the corner, he let out a startled yelp as he set off a motion-sensor light that lit up the backyard.

"Well," he muttered, "that's better."

He sensed movement to his left and turned to see a dark creature with glistening, sinister eyes emerging from a large boxy structure. The creature revealed a whole lot of long, sharp teeth, and then began to bark loudly as it ran toward him. It was a Rottweiler roughly the size of a buffalo.

Mr. Kraft felt his entire body vibrate with fear as he began to walk backward, groaning,

"Ooooohhh, boy." He tripped and fell on his back as the dog drew closer and its barking grew louder.

Mr. Kraft crawled on his back for a bit, then rolled over and crawled over muddy ground on all fours until he reached the gate, where he clambored to his feet. As he fumbled with the latch, he glanced over his shoulder and saw the dog closing in on him.

He knew he didn't have time to get the gate open, so he grabbed the top of the gate, which was a few inches taller than he, and pulled himself up. As Mr. Kraft was swinging his right leg over the gate, the dog buried its fangs into his coat and began to pull.

"Oh, no, no!" Mr. Kraft cried. "Down, boy! Down, Cujo! Stop it! Let go, come on, leggo! D-don't, uh . . . don't make me come down there! Do you know how much this coat cost me, dog?"

The dog growled and pulled, and Mr. Kraft fought to get over the gate, and then there was a great ripping sound as half the coat ripped away. Mr. Kraft tumbled over the top of the gate and landed on his back with a thunk.

He opened his eyes, but squinted when someone standing over him shined a flashlight in his face.

"Having a little trouble this evening, sir?" a deep, monotone voice asked.

"Well, I think I would use stronger words to

describe it," Mr. Kraft said, "but, yes, I'm having a little trouble."

"Mind standing, sir?"

Mr. Kraft stood and started to brush himself off, but found it was rather difficult to brush off mud. His robe was covered with it, and he'd lost one of his slippers. On top of that, all that remained of his coat were the shoulders and sleeves.

The flashlight was held by a police officer . . . a very large police officer standing under an umbrella. The officer ran the light up and down Mr. Kraft.

Smiling, Mr. Kraft asked, "Would you mind terribly if I shared your umbrella?"

"I'm afraid not, sir. This is an official police umbrella, not authorized for civilian use. And besides, I don't think the umbrella would make much difference at this point, sir. You're pretty wet." The officer did not smile.

"Yes, you're right about that. Well," Mr. Kraft said, grinning as he clapped his hands together once, "I should probably get back to my car and head for—"

"I don't see that happening right now, sir."

"Okay, I understand, you're wondering what I was doing in someone's backyard like that, but I can explain. You see, my secretary, Mrs. Mettwurst lives here. I had no idea she had Godzilla in her backyard, or I never would have gone back there. See, I'm the vice-prin—"

"Mettwurst?"

"Yes, you know the Mettwursts?"

"I know everyone around here, sir. Including the Mettwursts . . . who live across the street."

"Ah, I see." Mr. Kraft smiled bitterly and nodded. "That would mean I got the . . . the wrong house."

"You were planning to break into the Mettwursts' house, sir?"

"Yes, but it's been so long since I've been there, I—no! No, I wasn't planning to break in, I was just trying to—"

"Please turn around and put your hands behind your back, sir," the officer said, removing the handcuffs from his belt.

"Turn around? But I—"

"Just turn around, sir."

Mr. Kraft's smile disappeared quickly. "Does that, uh . . . does that mean I'm . . . in trouble?"

"Yes, sir, that's exactly what it means."

Chapter 11

☆

Sabrina went to school early the next day and went straight to the office. Mrs. Mettwurst was there, smiling apparently at nothing in particular.

"You look happy and well-rested, Mrs. Mettwurst," Sabrina said with a smile. Adrenaline was buzzing through her body, but she wanted to appear normal and calm.

"Oh, yes, Sabrina, very well-rested. I had some help yesterday evening and was able to catch up on all my work."

"That's good. Is Mr. Kraft in?"

"No, I'm sorry," Mrs. Mettwurst said, her smile growing even larger. "He hasn't come in yet."

"When do you expect him?"

"About thirty minutes ago."

"So you don't know when he's coming in?"

"Afraid not."

"I'll check back."

Sabrina left the office and headed for her locker. She almost ran into a woman who was hurrying out of the restroom.

It was Mrs. Mettwurst.

Sabrina gawked at the woman and, after a long silence, said, "Mrs. Muh-Mettwurst?"

"Hello, dear," the woman said, smiling. She started to walk away, but Sabrina reached out and grabbed her elbow.

"Wait, wait," Sabrina said. "Didn't I just see you in the office?"

"Oh, yes, no doubt. But I'm leaving now. Good-bye!" She turned and walked away, and Sabrina let her go.

At her locker, Sabrina got the book she would need for her first class, then turned around and went back the way she had come. She planned to wait near the office as long as possible—at least until the second bell—for Mr. Kraft to arrive.

As Sabrina passed the restrooms, another woman came out and headed for the front of the building.

Sabrina froze, stunned. "Uh, Mrs., um—" She cleared her throat and raised her voice. "Mrs. Mettwurst?"

The woman stopped and turned around, and, yes . . . it was Mrs. Mettwurst . . . again.

"Yes?" Mrs. Mettwurst asked with a smile.

"Um, didn't you, uh . . . just come out of that restroom?" Sabrina asked, feeling dizzy with confusion.

"Why, yes, I did."

"No, no . . . I mean a couple minutes ago . . . before you came out of the restroom." Sabrina put a hand over her eyes, shook her head hard, took a deep breath, and tried again. "I mean, you came out of that restroom a couple of minutes ago, and then . . . you came out of it again!"

"Well, not me personally," Mrs. Mettwurst said, "but I know what you mean. I'm on my way out now. Have a nice day, dear!" She waggled her fingers at Sabrina, then turned and headed for the front of the building.

Sabrina frowned and chewed on a thumbnail, eyeing the door of the restroom. Something wasn't right . . . again. She went into the restroom.

Three Mrs. Mettwursts stood at the mirror applying makeup and arranging their hair. Three identical Mrs. Mettwursts.

They hadn't noticed her yet, and she didn't want them to, so Sabrina turned and hurried out of the restroom. She jogged down the hall to the office, where she found another Mrs. Mettwurst behind the counter.

"Hello, again," Mrs. Mettwurst said with a smile.

Sabrina smiled and said hello, and then took a moment to choose the right words.

"You know, Mrs. Mettwurst, this might sound odd, but . . . since I left this office a little while ago, I've seen five of you."

Mrs. Mettwurst gasped and slapped a hand over her mouth. "I thought they'd left," she garbled into her palm.

"Well, I think they're on their way out, but . . . that's not the point, Mrs. Mettwurst. They're all identical replicas of you!"

"Sssshhhhh!" Mrs. Mettwurst looked around to make sure no one had walked in. "Yes, I know," she said. "I don't know where they came from, but last night, all of a sudden, there they were! Eager to help me with my work, ready to finish up all the stuff I'd fallen behind on, and happy to do it! I thought it was some kind of dream from being so tired and overworked, you know? I figured they would just sort of fade away after a while."

"Well, they haven't," Sabrina said. "I just left three of them in the restroom."

"Oh, dear. This could be . . . troublesome."

"Mrs. Mettwurst, you have to tell me where those duplicates came from!"

"Believe me, I would if I could! I couldn't believe it myself when they showed up. And they didn't even show up, really . . . I mean, they didn't come into the office, they were just, all of a sudden, here . . . out of nowhere. I didn't think they were real, but then I came in this morning and all the work was done. Like magic. . . ."

Sabrina rubbed her eyes, massaged her temples, then said quietly and very seriously, "Listen to me carefully, Mrs. Mettwurst. Have you recently come across an imitation leather pouch filled with something that looks like glitter?"

"Why, yes. Mr. Kraft gave it to me, and I got rid of it for him."

Sabrina's eyes widened. "Got rid of it?"

"Yes. He told me to give it to someone or other, and I did."

"Someone? Which someone? Who?"

"Well, it was, uh . . . let me think." Mrs. Mettwurst looked at the floor and stuck the tip of an index finger in her mouth as she thought. Suddenly, her head popped up and she smiled. "The dance committee!"

"Mr. Kraft told you to give the pouch to the dance committee?"

"Yes. He said they were complaining about not having enough glitter, so they might be able to use it. I gave the pouch to Ms. O'Connor, the home ec teacher. She's working with the dance committee, so I thought she'd be able to make good use of it."

So, Mr. Kraft didn't have the wishdust after

all! Sabrina took in a deep breath and let it out slowly through a smile. "You gave it to Ms. O'Connor. Okay, that's good. Is she in her office now?"

"Oh, no, I'm afraid not. Ms. O'Connor called in sick. There seems to be a nasty bug going around and she's got it. She won't be coming in today."

Sabrina buried her face in her hands and groaned. It was almost as if the pouch of wishdust was fleeing from her!

"Could you give me Ms. O'Connor's phone number?" Sabrina asked, lifting her face from her hands.

"I'm sorry, but that's privileged information," Mrs. Mettwurst said. "Ms. O'Connor can give it to you, and she can notify me with permission to give it to you . . . but other than that, it's privileged information."

"All right," Sabrina said, trying to smile. "Thanks for your help, Mrs. Mettwurst."

Sabrina left the office. She could get in touch with Ms. O'Connor on her own, but she'd need a private place to do it. A stall in the restroom usually worked for that sort of thing, but she was afraid she'd still find some remaining Mrs. Mettwursts in there.

Students were starting to pour in through the main entrance. Sabrina spotted Valerie and hurried toward her.

"Oh, Valerie, I'm so glad to see you!" Sabrina said sincerely.

"Wow . . . what'd I do?" Valerie asked, looking around rapidly, confused.

"You didn't do anything. I just need to talk to you."

The two of them walked together on the way to Valerie's locker.

"I need a favor, Valerie," Sabrina said.

"Sure, no problem. What is it?"

"When you get together with the dance committee today, I need you to look for something that's been given to them. By mistake, I might add."

"But I'm not on the dance committee anymore," Valerie said as she stopped at her locker.

"What?" Sabrina blurted out.

"No, not since that horrible mistake I made. I mean, think about it . . . I nearly had a yak at the dance, not to mention a musical group that sings only Latvian folk songs. Let's face it, Sabrina, I'm a failure when it comes to planning dances. I'm just no good at it."

"That's ridiculous! You made one mistake! That's all!"

"Apparently one's enough when it involves Latvian folk music and a yak," Valerie said, rolling her eyes.

Sabrina massaged one temple hard with her

fingertips as she asked, "So, Ms. O'Connor says you're no longer part of the dance committee?"

"I don't think Ms. O'Connor even knows about the Latvians yet," Valerie said. "I heard she's sick."

"So who said you're no longer part of the committee?"

"Libby, of course. She won't let me in the gym."

"But she can't do that! Ms. O'Connor is the one who put you in that position, and nobody but Ms. O'Connor can dismiss you from it!"

"Maybe so," Valerie said with a shrug. "But if Ms. O'Connor isn't around, Libby's the boss, and after what I did . . . let's face it, Sabrina, I really blew it."

Sabrina stepped in front of Valerie and put a hand on her shoulder. "Listen to me, Valerie, you have to get in there. Libby has my pouch. I mean . . . I think she has it. If she doesn't, then somebody else on the committee might have it."

Valerie pulled her head back and frowned. "Sabrina, aren't you getting a little obsessive about this bag of yours? Remember when you wanted me to get your rabbit's foot back from Libby? How much did I mess that up? Hmm? And this bag. I mean, you said there's not even anything in it."

Sabrina knew defeat when she saw it. She

stepped away from Valerie, and the two of them began walking side by side again.

"It's no big deal," Sabrina said. "I'll find it eventually, I guess."

"Yeah, Sabrina," Valerie agreed. "I mean, it's not like one little bag is gonna change the world or anything. Right?"

Sabrina forced a smile. "Yeah . . . right." There was a moment of silence between them, then, "Well, I've gotta go, Valerie. I'm, uh . . . supposed to meet Mark. See you in class!"

Thirty seconds later, Sabrina was huddled in one of Mr. Edgerly's utility closets, surrounded by mops and rags and buckets and jugs of industrial-strength cleaners.

"I need an open line and a dial tone,
    and put 'em both in a telephone."

Sabrina held out both hands, palms up, and produced a telephone. She picked up the receiver and said, "Call Ms. O'Connor." The phone dialed the number, and when Sabrina put the receiver to her ear, she heard the ring.

She got Ms. O'Connor's answering machine.

Sabrina called back a few times, hoping Ms. O'Connor would get frustrated with the ringing and pick up . . . but all she got was the answering machine. Finally she left a message: "Ms.

O'Connor, it's Sabrina Spellman. I know you're sick, and I'm sorry . . . but I think somebody gave you a little pleather pouch yesterday. It was full of something that looked like glitter, but . . . it's not. It's, um . . . well, it's a kind of experimental thing, see? The glitter stuff, I mean. But it's, um . . . it's been recalled because it's, uh . . . it's toxic! I, uh . . . I have an uncle who works in the lab that stuff came from, and he gave me a pouch of it, but then I lost it, and now it's been given to you, and now I—"

The phone was picked up at the other end.

"Sabrina?" Ms. O'Connor croaked. Her voice was very hoarse, and she spoke barely above a whisper.

"Yes, Ms. O'Connor?"

"I may be a very good cook . . . but I am not stupid. I know a crank call when I hear one. I'm very sick. I'll forget this on one condition."

"But this isn't a crank call! I'm trying to—"

"That one condition is that you don't call back. Good-bye."

Ms. O'Connor hung up.

Sabrina clenched her teeth and made an angry growling sound as she made the telephone disappear.

She left the closet and hurried down the hall toward the back of the building.

"Hey!" Mark called behind her.

She stopped and turned to see him jogging

toward her. For a moment, she forgot all about the wishdust and the numerous Mrs. Mettwursts, and she returned his smile as he approached. He didn't make her tingle like looking at Harvey used to do, but her heart did beat a little faster.

"Hey, I just realized something," he said. "We never really talked about our plans for tonight."

"I guess we didn't," Sabrina said as he took her hand.

"Well, I figured I'd pick you up at seven-thirty?"

"Sure, that'd be fine!"

"Good. I wasn't sure."

"You weren't sure? What, you expected me to walk to the dance?"

He laughed. "No, not that. I guess I'm just not very good at this sort of thing."

"Hey, listen, Mark . . . you're just fine at this sort of thing. Trust me."

He gave her a long look and said, "Thank you."

Then Sabrina remembered what she'd been doing before he showed up.

"Hey, I've gotta go, Mark," she said. "I'm, uh . . . supposed to meet Valerie. See you in class, okay?"

"Sure," he said.

Sabrina started to hurry away, but stopped. She turned back and gave Mark a quick kiss on the cheek. "See ya." Then she rushed out of the building and ran through the rain to the gym.

The gym had four entrances, and each one had a sign in front of it that read:

**THE GYM IS CLOSED TO ALL
BUT DANCE COMMITTEE MEMBERS.**

Sabrina knew she'd be caught if she walked through one of the doors. But surely there wasn't anyone in there so early in the morning. They couldn't be working on the decorations at this hour.

Sabrina looked around to make sure no one was watching, then waved her hand and sent herself into the gym in the blink of an eye.

She gasped when she found herself standing right behind Libby in the decorated gym.

Before she could eject herself from the gym again, Libby turned around.

"What are you doing here?" Libby asked. "I thought we'd gotten rid of the freaks when I kicked your pinhead friend Valerie off the committee!"

"Well, for one thing, Libby, Valerie is not a pinhead. She made a simple mistake!"

"Part of her simple mistake would've made a mess on the gym floor!"

"Look, Libby, I know I'm not supposed to be

here, but I have to ask you a question, just one simple—"

"Mr. Edgerly!" Libby cried. "Mr. Edgerly, we have an intruder!"

Seconds later the janitor was standing at Sabrina's side with a hand on her left elbow.

"I'm really sorry, Sabrina," he said, "but unless you're on the dance committee, you can't be in here." He began leading her to the door. "But don't worry, you can see it tonight. And it'll look all beautiful, I'm sure." He gave her a friendly smile as he pushed a door open and eased her outside of the gym. "You have a good day, Sabrina." He pulled the door closed.

Sabrina was tired of hunting down that pouch. In fact, she was exhausted. Suddenly she was no longer interested in finding that stupid wishdust. The only thing she was interested in was Mark's smile.

By the time Mr. Kraft arrived at school that day, all the students had left. That was fine with him, because he was still wearing his muddy bathrobe, one slipper, and what remained of his coat. He'd ended up spending more time in jail than he'd expected because his attorney was out of town, and Mr. Kraft hadn't been able to reach him by phone until about noon that day.

Mrs. Mettwurst was still in the office, but she was preparing to leave when Mr. Kraft entered.

When she saw him, her mouth dropped open, and she dropped a handful of folders to the floor.

"Mrs. Mettwurst!" Mr. Kraft cried. "Uh . . . which one are you?"

"I'm the original," she said with a smile.

"So, all those copies of you are gone?"

Mrs. Mettwurst's smile fell away, and she frowned deeply. "How did you know about them?"

"That's not important. Where are they?"

"Well, they're . . . gone! I figured they'd just sort of self-destruct, you know? Like that little tape recorder on the old *Mission: Impossible* TV show!"

"Fine, fine," Mr. Kraft said. "Look . . . I need to know where that pouch is . . . the one I gave you yesterday to give to the dance committee."

"I gave it to the dance commitee!"

Mr. Kraft closed his eyes and tried to gather his patience. "To whom did you give the pouch, Mrs. Mettwurst?"

"I gave it to Ms. O'Connor. But she didn't show up today because she's sick."

Mr. Kraft began rubbing his eyes with thumb and forefinger as he muttered, "Oh, how I wish I had that excuse."

"Where have you been, Mr. Kraft?" she asked in a shocked whisper. "And . . . what happened to you?"

He lifted his head and gave her a maniacal

grin. "Where have I been? You want to know where I've been, Mrs. Mettwurst? Well, I'll tell you." He chuckled. "I've been in jail. I was locked up with three thieves; four large, tattooed, and hairy motorcycle gang members; some smelly guy in a clown suit; and a flasher named Mort, who insisted he could hear the mother ship coming for us. And I have seen more than enough of *you* in the last twenty-four hours!"

Mrs. Mettwurst looked horrified as Mr. Kraft spun around and left the office.

The only thing he wanted to do was sink into a hot bath for a while, then take a long nap. Nothing else mattered to him right then. He would have to deal with the wishdust at the dance . . . because it looked like that was where it was going to show up.

"It still doesn't look right," Libby said, standing in the center of the gym and looking around at the decorations.

Sparkling drifts of plastic snow were piled in the corners, and there were two Styrofoam snowmen flanking the main entrance. The stage, where the band would play (whatever band answered her last-minute call to the college radio station), was made up to look like a frosty winter scene, and the tables that would hold the punch and snacks were covered with glittery tablecloths to simulate a surface of ice. Small artificial trees with winter-bare branches were set up here and there and strung with white twinkle lights, and glistening plastic icicles were suspended from silver streamers.

Still, Libby wasn't satisfied. She thought there should be more. It was pretty . . . but it still looked like a gymnasium. Libby wanted people to walk in and forget it was a gymnasium.

"It's looking really good, Libby!" Cee Cee said as she came into the gym. She carried more packages of streamers under one arm and something small in her other hand.

"It looks like a gym with trees," Libby said, frowning. "If only we had more glitter . . . a lot more glitter."

"Well, it probably won't be much help," Cee Cee said, "but I found this on Ms. O'Connor's desk." She handed over a small pouch.

Libby opened it and looked inside. "Wow," she whispered, "this is beautiful." She reached inside and scooped some of the iridescent glitter up in her hand. It was so pretty, it made her smile. She let it sprinkle gracefully from her fingertips as she said, "Gee, I . . . I wish we had enough of this stuff to cover the rest of the walls and the ceiling of the gym. . . ."

Chapter 12

☆

Mark called Sabrina at seven-twenty that evening to say he would be late. He said he was having car trouble and apologized three times before Sabrina interrupted him and said it was okay. He sounded so nervous, so guilty. Sabrina assured him she didn't mind, then went downstairs.

"Oh, Sabrina, you look beautiful!" Aunt Zelda exclaimed.

"That's such a lovely outfit, Sabrina!" Aunt Hilda added.

"Thanks," Sabrina said, smiling. "It's just a little something I conjured up." She twirled around. The sparkles in her black top reflected the lights in the kitchen. *Very cool,* she thought with satisfaction.

Salem trotted into the living room and hopped up onto the back of the sofa. "Nice outfit,

Sabrina," he said as he began to wash his face. "Do you think the dance will still be there when you arrive?"

"Very funny, Salem," Sabrina said with a sigh. "Thanks for the encouragement and vote of confidence."

"Well, who knows? If the wrong person makes the wrong wish at the wrong time, the whole school could turn into a theme park."

Salem wasn't far off. The random wishes of her schoolmates had been escalating all week. By Friday, lunch was a make-your-own-sundae party, Mr. Marsico's fourth period English class was reading movie novelizations, woodshop was turning out duck decoys, the second-string football squad had signed up to play intramural chess, and algebra class was being held from 11:05 to 11:08 A.M.

"Don't worry, I'm going to keep my eyes open for the wishdust," Sabrina said with resignation. "But I've had a rough week, and I'd like to have a little fun tonight."

"You're right, Sabrina," Aunt Hilda said. "You should enjoy yourself!"

"Yes," Aunt Zelda agreed. "Just . . . don't forget about that wishdust."

When Mark arrived, he presented Sabrina with a lovely bouquet of flowers. Aunt Zelda promised to put them in water. Sabrina and Mark walked under his umbrella to the car.

"What kind of car trouble were you having?" Sabrina asked.

"Well, it wasn't exactly car trouble," he said, starting the car. Once they were on the road, he said, "I was afraid the truth would sound too silly. See, my little brother's pet boa constrictor got loose in the car this evening and we couldn't find him."

"Boa constrictor?" Sabrina blurted.

"Don't worry," Mark said with a laugh. "He's safe and sound in his tank at home now."

"Good," Sabrina said with relief. She wanted to have fun, but as she'd promised her aunts and Salem, she had to keep her eyes open for the wishdust. The last thing she wanted to deal with that evening was a snake . . . or any other kind of animal.

Mark parked the car in the school lot and they hurried through the rain toward the gym. They could hear music playing inside and the sound of laughter.

Sabrina spotted a figure to their right heading for the gym as well. A familiar figure. Mr. Kraft.

Uh-oh, she thought.

Then she spotted several figures to their left, also heading for the gym. They were wearing odd hats and carrying large cases . . . and something very large was following them . . . something that walked on four legs.

"Uh-oh!" Sabrina said aloud.

"What's wrong?" Mark asked.

Before she could respond, she saw Mr. Kraft stop the other arrivals and say, "Hey, hey, who are you guys?"

Several male voices replied to Mr. Kraft . . . in a foreign language.

"The Frozen Tundra!" Sabrina exclaimed.

"Huh?" Mark asked, confused.

"The Latvian folk band . . . they were supposed to be replaced."

As Sabrina and Mark approached, Mr. Kraft was flailing his arms in frustration and said, "Don't any of you guys speak English?"

The Latvian band members stepped aside to let their large animal move forward.

Mr. Kraft let out a shrill shriek and stumbled backward. "Cujo!" he cried.

"It's a yak, Mr. Kraft," Sabrina said. "Look, I can explain this."

After taking a moment to compose himself, Mr. Kraft gave her a withering look. "Well, well, well. Miss Spellman. Imagine my complete lack of surprise to hear that." He looked at Mark and said, "And who is this . . . Darrin number one or Darrin number two?"

"Huh?" Mark said.

Sabrina quickly explained to Mr. Kraft about the Latvian band, then took Mark's hand and headed into the gym. "I'll be right back, Mr. Kraft! With someone who can take care of this."

She and Mark hurried inside, and Sabrina looked for Valerie as Mark closed his umbrella. Spotting her friend, Sabrina rushed to Valerie and told her the Frozen Tundra had arrived.

"Arrived?" Valerie cried. "But they were canceled . . . I thought!"

"They're outside right now," Sabrina said. "With their yak."

"Not exactly," Mark said, tapping Sabrina's shoulder. "Looks like the yak decided to come in out of the rain."

Sabrina and Valerie spun around to see the yak wandering toward the punch bowl. As others noticed the slow-moving, horned animal, a few alarmed screams rose, followed by laughter.

Libby ran by them shouting, "Why is there a cow in here?"

"It's a yak!" Valerie shouted after her. She turned to Sabrina and Mark and said, "I'll let her handle it. After all . . . I'm no longer on the dance committee."

Sabrina laughed as Valerie walked back to Lawrence Roddencone, who was wearing a tapeless pair of glasses.

As the band on the stage began a new song—a slow song—Mark asked, "Would you like some punch . . . or would you rather just dance?"

"Let's dance," Sabrina said with a grin. *Maybe the yak will eat Libby's dress. . . .*

The gym was beautifully decorated, as much

as Sabrina hated to give credit to Libby and her friends for anything. It looked like winter in some kind of fantasyland . . . like a picture on a Christmas card. The band was good . . . and they sang in English.

For all his self-deprecating talk, Mark was a good dancer and held her confidently in his arms.

The yak made a loud grunting noise, and someone screamed, "This buffalo is drinking the punch!"

Sabrina felt something wet on her head . . . then on her hand. She pulled away from Mark a bit and looked at the back of her hand. There was a drop of water there with tiny bits of ice in it . . . almost like . . .

Pulling away from Mark completely, Sabrina stopped dancing and looked around.

The Latvian folk band had come inside, and Mr. Edgerly was trying to shoo the yak away from the punch.

Falling gracefully on everyone in the gym was . . . snow. Real snow!

"Oh, no!" Sabrina said.

"Who wished for this snow?" Mr. Kraft shouted. "Everybody stop dancing! Stop the band! Nobody moves until I know who wished for this snow!"

Everyone began to look at Mr. Kraft as if he

were a lunatic. He climbed onto one of the snack tables and shouted again, "Who wished for this snow?"

"It's snowing," Mark said with amazement. "It's really snowing! In the gym!"

The wishdust is here! Sabrina thought, looking around.

Mr. Kraft was still on the table shouting for the band to stop playing.

The yak had nearly emptied the punch bowl.

The Latvian folk band was standing just inside the main entrance, some gesturing to the yak, others to the snow, all of them yammering in their native tongue.

There was some glitter on the tables, maybe that was it. Or maybe it was the glitter on the snowmen, or on the floor of the stage. She looked up and paid close attention to the glittery icicles hanging from the streamers. And then . . . she noticed something else.

The entire ceiling of the gym, including the beams, was covered with a sparkling layer of iridescent glitter. Beneath the ceiling, the top half of the walls were coated with it, too. It wasn't the kind of thing Sabrina could imagine the school allowing for a dance. It would have required very tall ladders and a whole lot of people, time, and glue to get all that glitter to stick way up there.

"Uh-oh," Sabrina muttered.

The snowfall became thicker as Mr. Kraft jumped off the table and hurried over to Sabrina.

"All right, Glinda, the Good Witch," he hissed. "Are you the one doing this? Did you find your wishdust?"

"Huh?" Mark said. He looked at Sabrina and asked, "What's he talking about?"

"Nevermind," Mr. Kraft said to Mark. He turned to Sabrina and said, "Well?"

Before Sabrina could answer the vice-principal, the snowfall stopped. But it was quickly replaced by something else.

Money. Crisp new ones, fives, tens, twenties, fifties, and hundreds began to flutter down over the dance.

Chaos broke out in the gym as people stopped dancing to pluck the bills out of the air. The band stopped playing, and the band members knocked over their drums and dropped their guitars as they dove from the stage to go after the money. The Latvian folk singers began to jump for the green slips of currency.

Having emptied one of the punchbowls, the yak headed for another, stopping to eat a few dozen hors d'euvres on the way.

"Oh, great!" Mr. Kraft snapped, burying his face in his hands. "I'm going to end up on *Hard Copy*—for all the wrong reasons."

Sabrina knew she had to do something immediately. She couldn't use her magic against the powers of the wishdust, but her aunts had told her she could use her magic to get wishdust. But in front of a gymnasium full of teachers and students . . . and Mark?

Water . . .

Suddenly, Sabrina remembered that the wishdust was made powerless by water! And if the sprinkler system had worked once . . .

With a twirl of her finger, Sabrina turned on the interior sprinklers. The money stopped falling almost instantly. Whatever money hadn't been snatched out of the air stuck to the floor.

There was even more screaming and shouting as everyone ran from the dance floor and headed for the doors.

Mark grabbed Sabrina's hand and said, "Come on, Sabrina, let's get out of here!"

"I'll be right behind you!" she shouted to be heard above the shush of the sprinklers and the noisy crowd. "I've got to talk to Mr. Kraft!"

But while everyone else was leaving the gym, Mr. Kraft just stood there muttering into his palms and shaking his head. The second everyone was gone, Sabrina waved a hand at the vice-principal and sent him to his office the fast way . . . by magic.

Ignoring the water that had drenched her beautiful dress, Sabrina looked up at the wishdust on the ceiling and walls of the gym. She pointed at it with an index finger, then slowly began to turn her finger around and around, faster and faster.

"Twirling and swirling, work up a wind.
Pull all the wishdust into your spin.
Bigger and bigger, with all the dust
Thunder and lightning, and rain if
you must.
Vortex to bag, carry it away
No grain of dust here can stay."

The sparkling wishdust began to come off the ceiling and walls and become caught up in a swirling vortex. Like a glittering tornado, the spinning vortex of wishdust grew steadily in size as more and more of the dust was sucked from the walls and ceiling.

Sabrina looked around frantically for something big enough to hold all that wishdust. She spotted one of the large garbage cans positioned throughout the gym. It had a heavy-duty plastic garbage bag in it. She rushed over to the can, dumped out the garbage, and removed the plastic bag. When she turned around and looked at the tornado of wishdust, though, she feared she was too late.

Along with the wishdust, the water from the sprinklers was being caught up in the vortex as well. A wind was building. Some clouds had gathered just below the ceiling of the gym. And a single bolt of lightning flashed, followed by a grumbly roll of thunder!

"Uh-oh!" Sabrina cried.

The gymnasium was developing its own weather system! Chairs and decorations were being sucked into the magic-made tornado, which was beginning to move back and forth in the gym, threatening to break through the walls and go outside into the rain!

"Willard Scott!" Sabrina shouted as she waved one hand.

The sprinkler system turned off and the clouds began to disperse.

"Al Roker!" she cried, waving the other hand.

The thunder and lightning stopped, and the wind died down to a harmless breeze.

Sabrina held the big plastic bag open and shouted angrily and with great authority at the spinning vortex of wishdust, "Now . . . in the name of the Weather Channel . . . get in here!"

It was all over in an instant. The noise stopped, the breeze was gone . . . and the plastic bag was bulging with soggy wishdust.

Sabrina let out a long, exhausted sigh. She was startled by a loud, wet, grunting sound.

As if nothing had been going on around it, the yak stood at one of the tables eating cupcakes, paper liners and all. An odd silence fell over the gym . . . interrupted suddenly by the sound of the main doors opening. One of the Latvian folk singers hurried in, talking rapidly and angrily as he went over to the yak. He grabbed one of the yak's horns and began pulling, stopping to clap his hands now and then. The yak moved slowly as it went with the Latvian folk singer, who continued to rattle off what sounded like angry diatribes, all the way back out the doors of the gym.

Sabrina was left alone. She conjured a pen and piece of paper out of the air, quickly wrote a note, attached it to the bag, and waved her hands. The bag disappeared in the blink of an eye.

Slapping her hands together to brush the whole thing off, Sabrina turned and left the gym to find Mark.

"Special delivery!" Salem called when a bulging green plastic garbage bag appeared out of nowhere in the middle of the living room.

Aunt Zelda and Aunt Hilda hurried into the living room as Salem walked around the wet trash bag, sniffing it. Aunt Hilda took the note off the bag and read it aloud.

"Dear Aunt Zelda, Aunt Hilda, and Salem . . . I finally found the wishdust! There's a lot more of it than before, and I'll explain it all. It doesn't work as long as it's wet, so please dry some off for me. I have some loose ends to tie up before we send the wishdust back. Thanks!"

"What a relief," Aunt Zelda said with a sigh.

"Yeah," Aunt Hilda said. "But . . . how do you dry off wishdust?"

Chapter 13

☆

Mark stopped his car in front of Sabrina's house and turned to her.

"I'm sorry things were so messed up tonight," he said. "We didn't even get to finish our dance."

"And we're both soaking wet," Sabrina said with a laugh.

"Um, if you'd like . . . we could go dancing tomorrow night. I mean, to make up for what happened tonight."

"Sure!" Sabrina said, her eyes brightening. "That would be great!"

Mark got out of the car with his umbrella, walked around to Sabrina's side and opened her door, then walked her to the front porch of the house.

"I'll call you early tomorrow afternoon," he said, "and we can decide when to get together."

Sabrina nodded. "I'll look forward to it. Thanks for tonight, though, Mark. I really had a good time . . . even though it got a little weird."

"Yeah, well . . . um, okay, uh . . ." Mark was very nervous again, fidgeting there on the porch.

"Yes?" Sabrina pressed.

Mark took a deep breath, let it out tremulously . . . then leaned forward and gave Sabrina a sweet, warm kiss.

"See you tomorrow," he said with a grin. Then he turned and hurried back to his car beneath his umbrella.

Well, well, well. And I didn't even wish for that!

Inside, Sabrina found Salem stretched out on the back of the sofa. He lifted his head and said, "Well, well . . . Cinderella returns."

"Where are—" Sabrina started to ask.

"Up here," Aunt Zelda called.

Sabrina looked up to see Aunt Zelda and Aunt Hilda each hovering in a corner.

"Great-Grandma's here!" Sabrina said excitedly.

"I'm in the kitchen, dear," Great-Grandma called.

Before going into the kitchen, Sabrina waved a hand and changed out of her soaking wet dress and into a comfortable pair of dry sweats. As soon as she walked into the room, Great-Grandma gave her a big grin.

"I knew you'd get that wishdust back, Sabrina," the old woman said. She was standing at the island with a small pile of dry, sparkling wishdust on the tiles in front of her. On the floor beside her stood the fat garbage bag of wishdust. "Zelda and Hilda said you needed to use some of the wishdust before I took it to the Council, so I dried some for you."

"Um . . . why are they being punished again?" Sabrina asked.

"Well, as soon as they got the bag of wishdust, they called me. Once I got here, I remembered how annoyed I was at them for getting you into this in the first place, so I put them back in the corners." Great-Grandma raised her eyebrows high and reached up to scratch her head delicately. "Besides . . . it's kinda fun."

Sabrina went to the pile of wishdust and picked up a pinch of it between her thumb and fingertip. As she sprinkled it onto the tile, she said quietly, "I wish Mr. Kraft would forget everything I told him about myself." She took another pinch of it and said, "I wish everyone who was at the dance tonight would forget all about the real snow, and all the money, and remember only that the indoor sprinkler system went off again." Another pinch: "I wish Mrs. Mettwurst would forget all about the copies she accidentally made of herself." Another pinch: "I wish those copies would disappear and never show up again." Another: "I wish everyone would forget about all the weird stuff that happened at school this past week because of the wishdust." Another: "I wish Leonardo DiCaprio, Neve Campbell, Winona Ryder, and Brad Pitt would forget all about showing up at school and their lives would go on as if it had never happened."

"Brad Pitt came to your school?" Great-Grandma gasped, impressed.

"I wish I had the wishdust pouch on my table right now."

The little, much-handled pouch appeared on the table. Great-Grandma picked it up and put it in her pocket.

She picked up one more pinch of wishdust, but this time she did not wish aloud. She closed her eyes and smiled as she thought, *I wish Mark and I could have a great evening together tomorrow evening.*

"Okay, Great-Grandma," Sabrina said. "It's all yours."

Great-Grandma looked at the pile of wishdust and said, "All right, then. Into the bag . . . every last particle of you!"

The sparkling dust swirled upward off the tiles and shot into the garbage bag. A second later a few stray specks followed the rest with a tiny glint.

"You know," Great-Grandma said, "before I go to the Witch Council, I have to go to the

Rummage Realm to pick up Salome Pettyjohn. I know she'll be there. She's always there, bilking people out of their money with one scam or another. So, Sabrina, would you like to go with me?"

"To the Rummage Realm?" Sabrina asked, eyes widening.

"Yes. Then we can go to the Witch Council and watch Salome sweat."

"To be honest with you, Great-Grandma, I'm not interested in ever going back to the Rummage Realm. In fact . . . I'd rather staple my upper lip to the side of the Bullet Train."

Great-Grandma tilted her head back and laughed. "Good for you, Sabrina. You've learned your lesson. You're a smart girl. You'll go far."

"I don't want to go far, Great-Grandma," Sabrina said, giving the old woman a hug. "I just want to go to bed."

About the Author

Ray Garton has been writing under the name Joseph Locke for years to conceal his true identity while secretly working for the government. After nearly losing his life in a tank filled with great white sharks while carrying out his most recent mission—to infiltrate the underwater fortress of a multi-gazillionaire megalomaniac bent on world domination—Garton retired from government service. He decided to write full-time under his own name. He now lives in California with his wife, Dawn, their four cats—Bob, Yuki, Lamont, and Oscar—and his two hermit crabs, H. P. Lovecrab and Andy Rooney . . . as well as a few exploding pens and laser-firing wristwatches left over from his years of foiling the sinister plans of evil geniuses all over the world.

Under the name Joseph Locke, Ray Garton has written two *Sabrina, the Teenage Witch* books—*Ben There, Done That* and the young reader novelization *The Troll Bride*—as well as *The Secret World of Alex Mack: Hocus Pocus,* and *Good Burger,* based on the hit movie. He's written nine other books for young readers, all thrillers, and is currently at work on his next novel.

THE HOTTEST STARS
THE BEST BIOGRAPHIES

☆ **Hanson: MMMBop to the Top** ☆
By Jill Mattthews

☆ **Hanson: The Ultimate Trivia Book!** ☆
By Matt Netter

☆ **Isaac Hanson: Totally Ike!** ☆
By Nancy Krulik

☆ **Taylor Hanson: Totally Taylor!** ☆
By Nancy Krulik

☆ **Zac Hanson: Totally Zac!** ☆
By Matt Netter

☆ **Jonathan Taylor Thomas:
Totally JTT!** ☆
By Michael-Anne Johns

☆ **Leonardo DiCaprio: A Biography** ☆
By Nancy Krulik

☆ **Will Power!
A Biography of Will Smith** ☆
By Jan Berenson

☆ **Prince William:
The Boy Who Will Be King** ☆
By Randi Reisfeld

 Available from Archway Paperbacks
Published by Pocket Books

Sabrina The Teenage Witch™

Salem's Tails

What's it like to be a powerful warlock, sentenced to one hundred years in a cat's body for trying to take over the world?

Ask Salem.

Read all about Salem's magical adventures in this new series based on the hit ABC-TV show!

#1 CAT TV

By Mark Dubowski

Coming in mid-July 1998!
Look for a new title every every month

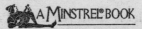 A MINSTREL® BOOK

Published by Pocket Books   1495